Rosie, John and
Putting Thin

Rosie, John and the God of Putting Things Right

Copyright © 2024 Celia Micklefield

Celia Micklefield hereby asserts the moral right to be identified as the author of this work of fiction

All rights reserved

No part of this publication may be reproduced, stored in a retrieval system, or transmitted in any form or by any means, electronic, mechanical, photocopying, recording or otherwise, without the prior permission of the author.

ISBN: 9798336445527

All characters in this publication are fictitious and any resemblance to real persons, living or dead, is entirely coincidental

ACKNOWLEDGEMENTS

Kingsley is the fictional town I created in my first novel, the dual timeline Patterns of Our Lives. In *Rosie, John and the God of Putting Things Right* I take readers back to the same Kingsley in the middle of the nineteen seventies.

I rely heavily on my memories of both Keighley and Bingley in West Yorkshire and apologise once more for messing about with their geography. I hope Keighley doesn't mind me borrowing the jewel box and Emerald Street. As for Myrtle Park in Bingley, I can't think of a better place for Rosie and John to have such a magical story.

Part One

Chapter One

Whenever I recounted our history together I always had to begin in the same place and tell it in exactly the same order. John wouldn't have it any other way. We were Rosie and John, in third person, not I and you. We were characters in the book he kept in his mind. He preferred it like that. He said it gave our story a sense of mystery and a kind of magic of its own. With his plate of chocolate biscuits beside him, he'd settle into his armchair, rest his head against the high back, cross one leg over the other, give me that boyish smile of his and say,

"Go on then, Rosie. Let's have our story."

I'd begin and every now and then he'd interrupt if I left out some small detail. It was important to remember it all, he said, because it was precious and it was our duty to keep alive the memories of those no longer with us who helped us on our way. He regularly surprised me by such deeply felt sentiments but he never lost his own childlike innocence nor his pride in the part he played in the story of Rosie and John and how we made magic happen in our home town.

1975

If there were a god of putting things right and just for his own entertainment he decided to come to Earth to choose a town to play with, it would never have been Kingsley. During Rosie's schooldays she saw only an ordinary town: familiar houses where people lived, from where they'd walk to school; where they had their tea when their mother came home from work and watched television before they went to bed. She didn't notice the time-worn buildings and dirty streets. That came later, after she'd grown up and experience had taught her lessons she didn't know she needed to learn.

Everything has changed since Rosie was ten years old. Kingsley looks completely different now but when she lived and played in the streets locals called the jewel box, the god of putting things right would have turned away and gone somewhere else. During Rosie's childhood years Kingsley was already deeply immersed in its period of re- development. In the old town centre a theatre that had once been a Victorian music hall was demolished to make way for construction of a shopping mall. Elsewhere, cobbled streets that could have been tourist attractions today were ripped up. Beautiful solid stone buildings - the old brewery, the dairy, shops, schools and chapels - many were torn from their hillsides and much of it replaced by concrete. But many old terraced homes remained.

Occupying their Pennine aspect Kingsley's regimented rows of smoke-blackened stone houses loomed over the town as if they were in command of it.

Squadrons of identical terraces fanned out in long marches to the heights while below them battalions ranked in tight streets laid siege to empty factories and defunct textile mills by the river. Kingsley's darkened dwellings scowled when the sun hit her rain-dampened roofs and pavements. They didn't glow in sunlight: they glowered.

Kingsley looked in on herself. In August, when surrounding moorlands burst into purple and pink, the town's streets looked blacker still as they hunkered down in their dark valley. Like an obstinate cat she showed her back to blue skies and purple heather. It seemed she never shone.

The god of putting things right would think he had too much to do here. No waving of a magical finger or puff of his life-enhancing breath would have the slightest effect on those solid buildings in their long, black rows. They were fixed in a time that no longer existed. Stubbornly they fastened to long lost days when Kingsley's factories and mills sounded their klaxons in celebratory toots and sirens signifying the end of another day's work, when there would follow a surge of workers filing through the streets like dark ants in their workday clothes, the soles of their shoes ringing against ironstone paving, the slick of their swarming a heady whiff of lanolin, engine oil and rubber.

During the nineteen seventies the sounds of Kingsley had become mostly traffic noises: the hiss of tires on wet tarmac; the rumble of wheels over cracks and bumps on the surface; the grind of windscreen wipers and the tick-click of vehicle indicators.

Most Kingsley folk went somewhere else for their daily work. The textile mills were closed and boarded, destined for demolition to make way for another supermarket or multi-storey car park. Or else they'd been bought by developers who transformed lanolin-soaked floorboards and metal-framed windows into loft apartments, where young executives could park their cars in the underground car park and have easy access to the road out of Kingsley each morning as they headed for their work in the city eighteen miles away.

By day, the town smelled of babies in pushchairs and cabbage leaves squashed in shopping trolleys left in wrong places. Of hairspray, deodorant and coffee shops. At night, there was chicken and burgers and curry and fish and chips. There was greasy litter on the pavements and the smell of beer and wine bars. The god of putting things right would pass by. He only wanted to play, anyway. It was entertainment he was looking for, not a lifetime's project.

His loss. If he had looked more closely, he would have recognised the kind of people who deserve a second look. He might have seen beyond the sad, black buildings and noticed the bright smile on a child's face in the little playground in the town's only park or the kindly pat on an aged person's shoulder from someone who cared. He might have noticed the colours of the flowers in that park and the young man who looked after them.

Chapter Two

John called his favourite colour corporation green. It was the colour of the doors on the council flats where he'd lived when he was a child. He often thought about those days. The bus route that used to take him to school went through several council estates on its way from John's side of town. There was a lot of corporation green. One of the estates, the newest one with semi-detached houses instead of blocks of flats, had a weird coral colour on the front doors or a bright blue or a shitty yellow alternating with the corporation green and he'd count the changeovers as the school bus rumbled along.

Coral, green, shitty yellow, blue. One. *Coral, green, shitty yellow, blue.* Two. And again. Three. And again. Four, until he was distracted by something in one of the bus queues and forgot where he'd got to and lost count.

There was no point in starting over the way he usually did when he lost his place in a sentence and went right back to the beginning to remember what he was going to say. You couldn't start over when you were counting things from the top deck of the school bus so he'd concentrate on not getting agitated that he'd lost count again and instead wait for the friendly green doors. He'd keep his eyes tight closed on a count of three. When he opened them again there should be a green door to look at. *Open. Close.* He timed it with the swish of the bus doors and the hiss of brakes.

Sometimes there were six counts of three between bus stops. Sometimes there were more. *Open. Close. Open. Close.*

He liked the view from the front seat on the top deck of the bus. He could see over the top of people's garden walls and practise the names of plants growing there. He took no notice of the boys who sat at the back and made a lot of noise. None of them were his friends so it didn't matter if they were saying unkind things. His mother had told him to ignore rude people so he did and she must have been right because the boys stopped calling him bad names eventually. Instead, they called him Spazza. John thought that was okay. One of the other boys was Barry and they called him Bazza, and there was a Sharon called Shazza, so the name Spazza made him feel like he was no different from any of them.

The noisy lot all got off the bus before John. They went to a different school, an enormous comprehensive school where there must have been hundreds of classrooms and thousands of people. John was glad he didn't have to go there. The noise would have been horrible and there would be too much pushing and shoving in the cloakrooms and in the canteen. And anyway that school had shitty yellow doors and windows.

Corporation green was his absolute favourite. It was a peaceful colour; it didn't shout like the other estate colours. He was glad his home had a green front door. It didn't matter what colour your curtains were, his mum used to say, because a corporation green front door

6

would go with everything. It was his mother who'd said the colours were *corporation*. He didn't know what the word meant when he first heard it. Now he knew it was just another word for things owned by the council.

The council owned everything. They owned the streets and the school and your house. So they could paint your front door whatever colour *they* chose. It seemed to John that if the council owned everything around them, they must own him and his mother too. Maybe he should be called *Corporation John*. That would make his mother *Corporation Iris*. But she was long gone now and John lived alone at Myrtle Court where the council had built what they called assisted living places. Arranged in blocks of four, the bungalow style, easy maintenance homes were just a short walk from the entrance to the town's park. He'd just had his twenty first birthday and he'd been given a raise at work. Funny it should turn out he'd end up working for the council.

In Myrtle Park where he worked the benches were corporation green. They were a comfortable shape, a friendly "S" shape with no sharp angles so they let your bottom go down and your thighs go up a bit so there was support beneath your legs. John had long legs. Very long legs. As well as Spazza, the kids used to call him *Spider Legs*, and he could laugh at that one because it was true: his long legs were covered in coarse black hair that grew onto them when he was about fourteen. His arms were long, too. In fact, everything about John was long including his head, ears and face. Long John, they could have called him, like in the story. Not Long John

Silver, though. Long John Spider Legs. Long John Spazza Spider Legs. Corporation Long John Spazza Spider Legs.

Each day John took his packed lunch to his favourite park bench close to the tuck shop kiosk. He enjoyed brief chats with all the passers-by and even knew some of them by name. Mr Eric was a favourite. Sometimes they'd sit together for a while but if there was nobody to talk to it didn't matter because there was plenty to look at.

There was a nice view from his favourite bench. On the upper level were most of the flower beds he worked on and below, on the lower level, the park sloped away and ran all the way down to the river. There were trees of every kind between the levels and in autumn the display was what his mother used to call magnificent. That was a word you didn't hear much these days: *magnificent.* Maybe most people didn't notice magnificent things any more. Maybe people were just too busy or sad or something to say that such and such was magnificent. John found magnificent things every day, but he kept the word to himself. It was too special to bandy about like it was only *cool* or *wicked.*

Just below John's favourite bench was the crown green for the bowling and off to the right was the little kiosk shop that sold hot drinks and sausage rolls in winter and ice creams and sandwiches in summer. The ladies served their customers through the tiniest window. The window was so small it was ridiculous. Jenny, one of the serving ladies was a big woman and she could hardly get her fat arm through the gap.

On the other side of the shop near the tennis courts and the swings were some animal enclosures. One was full of lovebirds and budgies. They twittered to each other all day long. Another housed hamsters and rabbits. John would save a piece of cucumber or a lettuce leaf and poke it through the bars. Sometimes he brought chunks of carrot.

Winter and summer he brought his lunch to the bench but one day in spring when the coral coloured tulips were poking through, John saw a child swinging her legs as she sat on his favourite bench. He walked right up to the little girl and the lady who was with her. He nodded and smiled at both of them and said a polite *Good morning* although he was annoyed they'd taken his favourite place.

"Lovely day," he said and the girl's legs dangled and swung about as her bottom slid all the way back into the curve of the "S". He remembered how that felt not to be able to reach the ground with your feet and how you would wonder what it might be like to be grown up and able to do it. After the lady had said her own polite *Hello*, he went to sit on the bench nearest the hamsters. *I'll get here earlier in future,* he thought as he took the lid off his sandwich box and gazed wistfully at his favourite seat.

John saw the child and the woman several times after that. He would nod and smile as they walked past him to find another bench because he'd got there first. He couldn't resist a satisfied grin at the way he'd got his place back to himself. Somehow his sandwiches always tasted better when he ate them on his favourite corporation green bench.

One day as spring was getting ready to turn into summer, when the coral tulips had gone over and shitty mustard yellow snapdragons were in their place, John was late to lunch. He'd gone to the shop first. Jenny, the lady with fat arms served him.

"And how are we this morning?" Jenny said. She leaned forward and put her arms on the counter behind the tiny window and it seemed to John she looked like a ship squeezed into a bottle: too big to be in there.

"I don't know how *we* are," he said. "*I'm* okay. How are you?"

"All the better for seeing your smiley face," she said. She stood upright and she laughed till her face and her arms jiggled. "What can I do for you today?"

"I forgot to bring a drink," John said. "I want to buy one. I will be thirsty soon. What have you got?"

She called out the names of drinks in cans and drinks in bottles and while he was making up his mind another customer came who Jenny knew. Their conversation went on so long it made him too late to choose his bench. The little girl was already there. He walked up to her with his can of fizzy drink in his hand. His stomach was rolling about inside him and he felt his cheeks growing hot. He wanted to shout, *that's my seat*. The girl saw him looking.

"Hello," she said. "Are you going to sit down? My mum is coming. Look, here she is."

John looked up. A woman was hurrying from the shop area towards them. It was the same lady who'd been talking to Jenny at the shop. He hadn't realised it was the lady who was the child's mother. Her hair looked different and she was in a different place. She wasn't *with* the little girl. People looked different in different places. John stood still and waited. The woman was bringing packets of crisps.

"Hello," John said. "Is it your lunchtime too?"

"That's right," the woman said as she drew close. She sounded out of breath from rushing and her eyes were a bit screwed up like when you didn't trust somebody or when you thought somebody was telling you lies.

"I don't like school dinners," the little girl said as she opened her crisps.

"So you're having a packed lunch with your mum. I never liked school dinners either," John said. "But I had to have them anyway."

"What are you having in yours today?" the girl asked as she nodded at John's sandwich box.

"Cheese. What have you got in yours?"

"Same as you. What's your name?"

"John."

"Hello, John. I'm Rosie."

The woman, the girl's mother pulled a funny face.

"Well, John," she said. "It was very nice to meet you, but we have to be going now," and she took hold of the child's hand and pulled her away so suddenly the girl spilled some of her crisps.

John sat down. He was glad the woman and the little girl had gone. He didn't want to share his favourite bench.

Chapter Three

Rosie Mirren wasn't like most other girls her age. Her mother told her she chose to give her the name Rosie because when she was born she screamed so loud and for so long her cheeks turned rose red with the effort she put into it. It was as if she'd announced her arrival with a surprising level of determination to make herself heard. It must have been an omen as she stayed outspoken ever since.

She came into the world in the mid nineteen sixties, a time when Rosie wasn't a popular girls' name. She didn't know that until she went to school and found herself among Lisas, Karens, Sharons, Debbies and Traceys and, for a time, she didn't enjoy having a name that made her stand out as unusual. It made her feel as if she should have been born in a different era.

You could say she was a loner, the kind of child always happy with her own company, filling her time with quiet leisure pursuits. She learned to read when she was only three years old so when she went to first school she spent much of the day occupying herself while Miss Hewitt helped the rest of the class.

By the time she left first years' education and made the move to middle school she had a reading age way beyond her year group and had already read most recommended children's classics from the school library. When she wasn't reading she was painting or sitting by herself watching television. You'd think she ought to have felt lonely but it never occurred to her that she was any different from most girls her age.

She was an only child and spent a lot of time daydreaming. Without siblings to share games and, living as she did in a street where there were no other children, her imagination took the place of playmates. She made alternative worlds from scraps of ideas: an old pair of heavy curtains thrown over the table made a tent underneath where she'd pile up cushions to create an enticing, darkened space for telling fortunes and granting wishes to her toys.

People often said she had an old head on young shoulders and that's a strange thing for any young child to overhear. She could have seriously frightened herself making mental pictures out of that saying. Trying to imagine what she'd look like with an old face, she'd stare in the mirror over the mantelpiece, forcing herself not to blink until her sight blurred. She hoped the face staring back at her might magically develop wrinkles but the face only went out of focus and she had to blink to stop her eyes from stinging. In any case, her young-old head understood what they meant. The fact is, she did spend much of her young years in the company of adults so it's not so surprising.

Rosie used to enjoy wondering what it might be like if there really was a magical being who could grant wishes. She'd sit in her home-made tent under the table and conjure him up. Like a genie from a bottle or an old fashioned oil lamp he or she would come at her bidding and solve all the little problems in her young world. But she knew even then you mustn't be greedy. She'd seen

Aladdin on television and remembered what happened to his uncle.

She must have had a lively imagination to fabricate such thoughts of putting the world to rights. Even as a child she knew it would take some special kind of alchemy to correct the wrongs she perceived and how in her fancies she'd try to make magic around her, to make everything better for the small group of important people in her world: her mother who always looked troubled and tried to hide it; old Eric who lived at the end of their street and liked to call himself her honorary grandfather; Jenny who worked at the tuck shop in Myrtle park and, latterly, for John who became her new best friend after their first meeting in the park and who wasn't able to concoct wizardry for himself.

Rosie was a serious child because, even though she held on to the fantasy of a god of putting things right, she had the insight to realise things were bad enough to need change. She judged her world through her child's eyes and, naturally, the way children think, the necessary modifications should have been as innocently simple as clicking her fingers and - *hey presto* - everything would be fixed. Besides, didn't she live in Emerald Street? The great Wizard of Oz lived in the Emerald City and, in her childlike way, Rosie took this as a sign.

Number seventeen Emerald Street was in a row of identical stone terraced houses. Older than the terraces climbing surrounding hills, the dwellings had undergone several refurbishments since their original layout of a simple two up- two down. Now they had a bathroom upstairs and where there used to be an open range in the kitchen there were now units with worktops and plumbing for a washing machine. The terraced houses were part of what locals called *the jewel box*, streets named after precious stones. Ruby Street was first, then Emerald, Sapphire and Pearl and Opal, all running off at right angles to the main road which cut the town in half.

There was a time when the stone houses would have been golden and clean. Now, blackened by more than a century of smoke from their own coal fires and from chimneys at the textile mills in the valley, the rows of former workers' homes stood like upright dominoes with clean white painted window frames instead of spots. At the front of each house a small square patch of green struggled to look like a garden and at the back a stone-slabbed yard housed a small outbuilding, dustbins and washing lines.

If they'd ever been considered precious there was nothing remarkable about them now. They were stout little houses, designed for the solid people of the north, hard-working types in the main, the sort of people others called the *salt of the earth*. These were the people of bygone days, men and women, who worked with their hands to make things in mills and factories until the sirens sounded and, though they lived limited lives of work and penny-pinching, they still retained the good humour to refer to their squat homes as the jewel box.

Tenants now worked in local services in supermarkets or in the retail mall that had sprung up out of the desecration of the old town centre. There was a post office and hairdressers, bakeries and butchers, cards and gift shops to serve the people of Kingsley and there were offices and wine bars and one cinema. Industry had left. In its place satellite businesses occupied small units where you could choose a new washing machine, carpets for your living room or vinyl flooring for your kitchen or bathroom. Chain stores filled the high street and the first of many charity shops spilled out onto the pavements so that they looked like a bazaar with baskets overflowing with cast off books and videos.

At number seventeen Emerald Street the lady of the house had finished her shift at the nearby supermarket and her kitchen was full of good smells. The table was set for two and there was going to be cake for afters. She was plating up chicken in a creamy sauce with rice, a ready meal bought with her staff discount, but her staccato movements were as if her hands were agitated.

"Come to the table, Rosie now, please," the woman called.

"Five minutes."

"No. Not in five minutes. Now."

"I'm not hungry."

"You must be hungry. You hardly ate any of your sandwiches today."

"That's because you made us leave the park. And I spilled my crisps."

"Rosie. It's ready now. Stop arguing. Turn the television off and come to the table."

"But this is my favourite programme."

Rosie's mother marched into the living room and turned off the television with an annoyed flourish. If her hands could have spoken they'd be yelling something hurtful. Her face was tight too and underneath her eyes were dark arcs. Rosie obeyed and stood up from the sofa. She followed her mother into the kitchen and sat at the table.

She doesn't understand about magic, Rosie thought. She picked up her knife and fork and began to eat but she couldn't stop herself from voicing the question on her mind.

"Mum?" she said. "Couldn't we have our tea at a different time?"

"No, we couldn't have our tea at a different time just so we can fit in with your television programmes. It doesn't work that way." Her mother's tone was firm but gentle enough for Rosie to press further.

"Well, couldn't it work that way just sometimes?"

"Rosie. It's not all about *you*, is it?"

Rosie knew her mother didn't expect an answer. She gave in. Her mother had *that* face on. There was no point in trying to explain about the mystery of magic and how if you don't believe in it, you'll never get to see any. Like in *Peter Pan,* you have to believe in fairies or Tinker Bell will die. Everybody knew that. Even the adults joined in shouting out *I believe in fairies* the last time they went to see a pantomime when she was very small.

That was when Rosie still had a dad, though. He'd surprised Rosie and her mum with a mystery night out and drove to the city without telling them where he was taking them. He *was* magic, her dad. He'd proved it. He disappeared one day in the family car and never came back and if that wasn't a kind of magic Rosie didn't know what it was. But that wasn't good magic. She hadn't seen a pantomime since, except for re-runs of old ones on television, and it didn't matter that she'd seen them all before. Knowing the story and what happened next became part of the magic of it. The good feelings that happened to you the first time you saw it were like happy memories and they came back when you saw it again to re-create the contentment of having had a good time. These days they didn't go anywhere much at all, really. Her mother said it was because there wasn't enough spare money to pay for trips away or days out somewhere.

So television programmes were Rosie's journeys to somewhere different. You could be a princess or a wild adventurer or almost anything at all when you slipped away into television land. And the best programme of all was the old one where the lady wiggled her nose and made magic things happen. Rosie thought it would be wonderful if she could do that. If she could *really* make magic happen instead of pretending she could, she'd conjure up something other than cheese in Myrtle Park John's sandwiches just so she could see his surprised face. That would be one of the best things about being

18

able to do magic, she thought. Doing something for somebody else would be so much nicer than just doing it for yourself. She'd make the sun come out so people's washing would dry. She'd magic extra chocolate cake and biscuits in the empty tin. She'd make flowers blossom in everybody's front garden so that bees and butterflies would come. Most of all she'd like to do some magic for her mother. Something that would make her smile sometimes.

Chapter Four

Jenny pulled off her thick Arran cardigan and hung it on a peg behind the tuck shop door. The day had started fresh and breezy and she'd needed the extra layer on her walk from home into work. The spiteful wind whistled across those Pennine hills and came back round again as if it didn't ever want to leave and what might look like a beautiful early summer day could take you by surprise. She sometimes called it a lazy wind.

Can't be bothered to go around so it goes straight through you she'd say to people in bus queues on the hill down into town. In the bus stop shelters there'd be mothers with babes in pushchairs wrapped up like little woollen bundles and wearing cute hats with ears.

And this is supposed to be summer, one of them might answer and they'd laugh together as if it was the first time they'd considered it although everybody knew you couldn't trust a Yorkshire summer day not to go and spoil itself. So you got yourself prepared. You carried a fold-up umbrella in the bottom of your shopping bag, just in case, and you said things like *it always rains when you forget your umbrella* or you'd tap your bag and say, *I've got my umbrella. It won't rain now.*

There were hundreds of Yorkshire sayings. Jenny knew them all. And it didn't matter how many times a person might have heard them, they'd still laugh and come back with the appropriate response.

Jenny didn't bother with the bus on the way into work. *I'll walk as long as I still can* she'd say if you asked her but the truth was she enjoyed the walk downhill into the valley. From where she lived you could see right across to the other side of the river where the posh houses were on the south facing hillside, built after the smoke from factory chimneys had been banned but before Kingsley had fallen into its slump. Those fine, detached houses had clean walls and red-tiled roofs and they were all surrounded by lovely gardens with big, mature trees. The folk who lived in the posh houses were probably all retired now, solicitors and accountants and the like, Jenny imagined. They'd have big cars in their garages and a gardener to look after their lawns. Anyway, she reasoned, what was the point of living in Kingsley's one desirable location when the view from there was the other way across the valley to Jenny's side with all its defunct mills and council estates?

No. Jenny had the better deal. The better view. And with her hand knitted Arran cardigan protecting her back from the malicious hilltop wind she ambled along past the bus queues, down past the rows of tightly-ranked houses, down further past the old mill chimneys and entered the centre of town from just behind the cinema. By this time the wind was less fierce. Then she crossed the main road, passed by the *jewel box* and on through the gates of Myrtle Park. It was a gentle, easy, downhill walk. It was a different matter at the end of her working day when her legs ached and she couldn't wait for a sit down. Then, the bus was a welcome haven with its convenient stop at the end of her street and a steady walk on the flat to her home.

The tuck shop in the park was always cold first thing in the morning. Even through the hottest days of summer, stepping inside was like going into a cold storage room. The building had been a keeper's lodge at one time, built from the same heavy stone as the big main residence which now housed a museum at the other side of the park. Six inches thick those walls were. They did a good job of keeping out draughts but took an age to warm through in sunlight.

What had been the sitting room was now a storeroom with floor to ceiling metal shelves on one wall and two chest freezers and a fridge on another. One corner of the room was boarded off for a toilet. The kitchen was her workspace and, jutting out at ninety degrees from the building, the adjoining lean-to walk-in pantry with its small window became the serving hatch which locals liked to call the kiosk. Originally there'd been shelving on both sides of the pantry. The upper shelves were wooden. The bottom shelves were made of enormous slabs of stone, secured within the walls themselves. With permission from the council Jenny had one side of shelving removed to give her more space to serve customers at the window. A reclamation company was happy to come for the stone slab. The other slab she kept. It was a good height to keep the cash box.

Jenny put her bag on the chair by the sink and rolled up her sleeves ready to begin her day's work. She switched on the lights, checked the water heater and by the time she'd got the urns on and the sandwiches prepared the sun had moved around and hit the little kiosk full in the face. Even the small window was enough to warm the place up but the sun got in her eyes when she was serving customers. She stepped outside to wind down the awning.

"Good morning, Jenny. And how are we today?"

John was pushing a wheelbarrow full of clippings on his way to the compost heap behind the animal enclosures, up by the park wall. Jenny smiled. John was using her own words again. He even copied the way she said them.

"Feeling the heat, now, John. Feeling the heat."

"It's a beautiful day."

"That it is. Have you much work laid on?"

"Laid on what?"

"Have you much work *to do* today?"

"I always have plenty of work to do, every day."

He was in one of his literal moods. No matter. He meant no harm.

"Where's Donna?" John asked.

"She's not coming in today, love. Had to take their Jason to the dentist."

"Been eating too many sweets?"

"Maybe. Have you remembered your drink today, John?"

"Yes. Thank you. I have to go now." And he pushed off on those long, gangling legs of his, his long arms stretched out in front of him and a huge grin on his long face. Jenny could hear him muttering under his breath.

Feeling the heat. Feeling the heat.

She knew it wouldn't be long before she heard those words coming right back at her. *Poor lad*, Jenny thought. *Life must be such a struggle for him.* Such a pity his mother hadn't lived to see him getting on with his life. She'd have been so proud of him holding down a job working for the council.

She was a lovely woman, was Iris. She adored her boy. Loved him to bits. She'd come to Kingsley from the West Indies somewhere to take up a cleaning job in the hospital when she was not much more than a kid herself. Life in Yorkshire must have been hard for her, too, in those days. Iris never said too much about it but Jenny knew enough to work out how things had gone for John's mum.

John was the result of a short affair with some no-good who'd treated her badly. To put it crudely, he'd simply fancied a taste of something different. That's how it looked to Jenny. From the things Iris did say about him Jenny thought he hadn't much cared about her at all. Iris had had stars in her eyes. He'd only wanted one thing. When he found out she was pregnant he'd done a disappearing act. Jenny found out later he'd got himself a job at the new oil refinery down south, somewhere near Southampton so it was obvious Iris would never set eyes on him again. He never contacted her. Never wanted to know whether she'd kept the baby. Didn't want anything more to do with her. She gave her baby her own surname, Grant. And Iris had forged a life for herself and her awkward boy.

I know he's different, she'd say. *But we're all different. Aren't we?*

The strength of the woman. She ignored suggestions from his schoolteachers that John should be assessed.

Why do we need to put a label on him? she'd say and carry on loving him. Until one day when he'd reached puberty and was coming out of the bathroom looking for a towel, naked as the day he was born, innocent as you like.

Neither Iris nor Jenny knew what macro-orchidism was and how that affected a young lad's growth. Iris had thought her son must have tumours in his testes and took him to see the doctor. Appointments with consultants at the hospital followed. John was taken to see so many different specialists his mother thought they would never find the answer to his unusual growth. After months of tests and examinations they were finally given an answer. Jenny helped Iris to look it up in a medical dictionary at the library. Neither of them had ever heard of the neurologist James Martin and geneticist Julia Bell who were the first to identify a fragile site on the X chromosome. They didn't know that Martin-Bell Syndrome, which became called Fragile X was the condition causing John's unusual development.

Chapter Five

Kingsley was full of people like Jenny, Rosie and her mother. Ordinary people going about their daily lives. Getting up in the morning and doing what they had to do. Coping through the day with their Yorkshire saws and sayings. Laughing when things went well. Laughing harder when they didn't.

Only, you never got to see what was going on inside. It didn't do to complain. Life was sometimes a struggle for most people so what was the point in talking about it? That only made things worse. Talking about troubles made them more real. Giving them voice made them larger than life, gave them too much importance. The people of Kingsley, like the town itself, turned their backs on worry and ignored it. They made jokes about it instead.

Rosie's mother, Linda had a way of coping with the day without humour. Since her husband had abandoned her and their daughter she had set her face with a look of grim determination and decided to keep it there. Cheerfulness left number seventeen Emerald Street the day that *he* went. Linda did not allow herself to feel any sense of joy in small pleasures the way she used to.

There was nothing to be gained in smiling at birds feeding from the grease balls Rosie hung on an iron hook in the wall in the rear yard. There was no satisfaction in admiring flowers in Myrtle park, no sense of contentment from any small task well done. Feeling anything other than resolute meant she would have to relax, open herself and her heart and become vulnerable to more helpings of heartache. Her firmness of purpose was her defence against the pain. Nothing was to be allowed to hurt her ever again as much as his rejection of her and their daughter.

She'd ingested the early devastating pain of his leaving and taken it deep inside her. It had burned its way into her stomach and sat there like so much acid blistering her insides. It had become part of her. It was there, burning in her eyes, searing the set of her mouth, scorching her hands and fingers. Always alert, always on the lookout for the next surge of pain, she kept herself in readiness, her eyes wary, her mouth tight, her hands busy. These were her charms against ill fortune, like the folded umbrella in the bottom of a shopping bag to ward off rain.

Rosie was too young to understand all this. All she could see was that her mother must be sad. And tired. Her work at the supermarket made her very tired. The child recognised signs of it in her mother's eyes, in her slow walk and the way her head sometimes seemed too heavy for her neck. When her mother came home from her day's work, Rosie could tell straight away whether her own bedtime would be an early one. It wasn't that her mother was cruel or even unkind. She was just tired. That's all it was. Often she seemed too tired to answer questions. She was too tired even to talk, sometimes.

When her mother was working Rosie stayed with a neighbour, Eric, the old man who lived at one end of Emerald Street. Linda had written a letter to Rosie's school giving Eric permission to collect Rosie at the end of the school day until her shift at the supermarket had finished when she would come to collect her daughter from Eric's house. That was okay. It was only like having a grandfather come to meet you and, anyway, that's what other people thought he was.

Eric's house had the same number of rooms as Rosie's but everything was the other way around. When you went in the front door, the rooms were on the right hand side and the staircase went up the left. She could never make up her mind which way round she liked it best.

Rosie thought Eric must be ancient. His hair was thick, wavy and pure white, like Father Christmas, and that was a good description of him even if he didn't have the beard to go with it. A kind man, very generous with his time, he liked playing board games and cards. He had a pile of children's games that had belonged to his own family before they all moved away to another country. There wasn't a Mrs Eric. She had died so Eric was on his own. He could do everything a mother does. He did all his own cooking and cleaning and looking after the house. Sometimes Rosie thought he was better at it than her mother was because everything always smelled nice at Eric's house and his washing was always ironed before he needed to wear it.

Sitting on Eric's sofa together with the board between them, Rosie had been playing a game of snakes and ladders with him. She knew he'd let her win but didn't let on she knew and pretended to be surprised and pleased.

"I win. I win," she said and clapped her hands.

Eric smiled and said, "Well done, young 'un. Well done to you. You beat me fair and square."

He got up and went into the kitchen and asked Rosie to follow him. He lifted the lid of the cake tin he kept on the kitchen work top.

"Don't tell your mum," he said and put out two chocolate muffins, "and make sure you eat all your tea later."

They were the biggest muffins Rosie had ever seen, wrapped in waxy, chocolate brown paper and bulging with chocolate nibbles.

"Did you make them?" she said.

"Not these ones, no. They were on special offer so I thought we'd have a treat."

"Eric?"

"Yes?"

"You know when you go in Myrtle Park?"

"Yes?"

"Well, do you know that man who does the flower gardens by the shop?"

"John? Yes, I know John. Why?"

"What's the matter with him?"

"What makes you think there's something the matter with him?"

Rosie struggled to find the right words.

"Is he . . .erm . . .lonely?"

She watched Eric think carefully about his response. His eyes scrunched and he bit at his top lip.

"I don't know if he's lonely, Rosie. You'd have to ask him."

29

"Mum doesn't like me talking to him. She pulled me away from the park the other day. Why doesn't she like me talking to him? Because, I think, when somebody is lonely you should talk to them then they won't be lonely any more."

"Eat your cake."

"Eric!"

"What?"

"Grown ups always do things like that to put you off when they don't like what you're saying. I want to know what's the matter with John."

Eric fiddled with crumbs on his plate.

"John is . . . different," he said.

"We're all different," she said. "Some people are tall, like John. Some people have cheese in their sandwiches and some people have meat. Some people have red hair and . . ."

"All right, all right," Eric said. "That's enough of that. Now, let me see, how shall I explain this? John is different from other young men his age because he . . . because . . ."

"Because he's more like a child my age?"

Eric reached out and stroked her hair. He was smiling still and his face was very kind. "How did you work that out?" he said.

"I don't know. I just know, that's all."

Rosie sighed as if she'd known all along that she was right and took a huge bite from her chocolate muffin.

Chapter Six

A few days later Eric was hanging out his morning washing. There was a fresh breeze and no sign of rain clouds, an excellent day for bedding. He liked the smell of bedsheets dried outside; it reminded him of the times his wife would wait for such a day to launder bed linens from the washing basket, how that sweet, fresh air aroma would bring a smile to her face as she brought them back indoors. He paused on the back doorstep to think more on it.

He often imagined her face. That was easy to conjure up: he had photographs of her in every room to remind him. But her voice? That was gone. Gone forever. Still, he tried to remember the music of it, how when she was impassioned about her favourite subjects her voice would rise to a higher pitch and he was still smiling to himself when there was a sharp rap at the front door. He went to see.

"Hello, Eric. Have you got a minute?" It was Linda, Rosie's mother. She had a jacket thrown loosely over her working uniform.

"Come in. Come in," he said. "Have you time for a cuppa?"

She said she'd have coffee before she went into work. She was on a later shift and would be along later to collect Rosie at about six.

"It's Rosie I'd like to talk to you about," she said, settling into a chair in Eric's kitchen.

"Oh, yes? And what's she been coming out with now?"

Linda brushed imaginary lint from her sleeve and took a deep breath.

"Well," she said, "it's to do with that young man who works in the park. I was wondering whether she might have talked to you about him."

Eric brought coffees to the table and sat.

"Ah," he said. "Hmm. She was chatting about him the other day."

"What did she say?"

"She wanted to know if I thought John was lonely."

"Is that all?"

"Pretty much. It seems to me as if she'd like to help him not be lonely. I think she'd like to be his friend."

Eric noticed Linda take another deep breath, as if she were guarding her words. She cleared her throat and took a moment before she composed herself and spoke again.

"I don't think it's appropriate for them to be friends, Eric."

She folded her hands on her lap and gave him a look that said that was the end of the matter. There would be no negotiation.

"I think you're wrong, dear," he said and his use of the endearment shocked him a little. It had obviously surprised her, too. Her eyes widened and her mouth fell open. But Linda and young Rosie felt like family to him now. Why shouldn't he speak in the way he would speak to his own? She held his gaze and waited for him to continue.

"John has a genetic condition, Linda," he said. "Something he was born with. It means he's had problems all his life. It's something to do with chromosomes getting mixed up." Her hands unclasped and she shifted in her seat.

"I knew there was something," she said eventually, "but I wouldn't have been able to give it a name. Chromosomes, huh? You mean, like in Down's Syndrome?"

"I guess so. Something like that. It's not the same as Down's Syndrome but I remember it was about unbalanced chromosomes. I don't know any more details."

"He doesn't have that kind of appearance, Eric."

"Not in the way you mean but it affects his physical appearance, certainly. You've seen how long his face and limbs are and the heaviness of his jaw." He meant to continue but Linda seemed agitated.

"How do you know that's what it is?" she said. "How can you be certain?"

"It was Jenny who told me. You know, Jenny at the tuck shop kiosk in the park. John's mother was a friend of hers."

"Was?"

"She died. Oh, a good few years ago. I'm not sure when. John lives by himself but I think he has a social worker who checks in on him every now and then. He has one of the new assisted-living homes at Myrtle Court near the park entrance. There's a warden, somebody just to keep an eye on things. Make sure everybody is okay."

"I thought those places were meant for frail and elderly people," Linda said. "John isn't either. I've seen him working in the flower beds. He looks as strong as an ox."

"Yes, he's fit enough for the work, Linda, but when it comes to everyday living I think there was nowhere else for him to go. He's too old for a children's home and too young for residential care. He gets some financial support from the council, I think. He won't earn much for the work he does in the park. It can't be easy for him managing on his own. Apparently he makes himself useful looking after other residents' gardens and running errands."

Linda's expression changed. Eric saw her eyes soften. Her shoulders relaxed and she chewed at her bottom lip.

"Well," she said, "Rosie's been saying much the same thing at home, about John being lonely. She notices things like that. We used to always have a packed lunch in the park. Rosie doesn't like school dinners, you know, and I've usually managed to arrange my own lunch break from work to coincide with hers. Except for when I'm on late shift then she has to eat hers at school. They've a table set aside for pupils with packed lunches . . ."

She stopped talking as if she'd lost the thread of what she intended to say or maybe as if she didn't know how to say it.

"Go on," Eric said.

"I stopped taking her into the park. John was always there. He always seemed to be hanging around

34

whenever I took Rosie in there. Wherever we sat down, there he'd be. It just didn't feel right that he wanted to talk to a ten year old."

Eric slapped his thigh and said, "Have I missed her birthday, Linda? I thought it was next week."

"It is."

"I don't know what to buy for her."

"Eric, there's no need."

"Oh, but there is. I'm an honorary grandfather. Except I'm a bit out of touch about what young folk like these days." He got up and went to open one of the drawers in the kitchen units. "What would she like?"

"We can't always afford what she'd like, Eric."

"Well, tell me what she needs."

"Pyjamas."

"Oh, I'd be no good at choosing." He reached in the drawer for his wallet and took out a ten pound note.

"That's far too much, Eric."

"So get her some other treat as well, then," he said as he sat back down at the table. "Who else have I got to spend a bit of money on? Now don't you be worrying yourself about young John. He's only a lad in his thinking, you know."

Linda shook her head. "Eric, he doesn't look like a lad," she said. "He's a fully grown man. He's strong. I suppose I was suspicious of his intentions."

"I don't think you need worry about that," Eric said with a sigh. "John would never harm her. He wouldn't hurt a fly. He doesn't have it in him."

"You can't possibly know that for sure, Eric." Her voice had hardened again.

Eric drained his cup and set it down. He leaned forward across the table and lightly touched the back of Linda's hand.

"Look here," he said. "Where is the harm in having your lunch together in the park? If you don't mind me saying, it seems to me that *you* are the one who needs to come to terms with your own discomfort around John. Rosie seems to be perfectly comfortable in his company."

She slid her hand from beneath his, stood up and fastened her jacket. She moved toward the door.

"I have to go now, Eric," she said. "I don't want to be late for work. Thank you for the coffee."

"Have I offended you?" Eric said.

She turned to face him.

"No," she said. "You haven't offended me. You've made me realise something about myself, Eric. That's all. And it's made me feel uncomfortable. Sometimes it's hard to face up to your own prejudices."

Eric held open the door for her and patted her shoulder.

"Everything's going to be all right," he said.

"I hope so," she said. "But you must understand, we still have to be careful."

She stepped outside and strode down the street. Eric watched as she hurried away.

36

Chapter Seven

Rosie bounded down the stairs two at a time on the sunny morning of her tenth birthday. She'd been secretly peeping in the cupboard under the stairs the night before and seen what she wasn't supposed to see: packages in colourful paper, all shiny and inviting. When she ran into the living room, the parcels were on the sofa.

"Mum," she called. "Can I open them before I go to school?"

Linda, tea towel in hand, came in from the kitchen to watch.

"Yes. Be quick. Breakfast's ready."

There was a pair of new pyjamas, some sweets, some fancy gel shapes to put in the bath and a large, tightly wrapped box. She couldn't wait to open it. She tore at it.

"Roller boots!" she yelled as the wrapping fell away. "Fantastic. Thank you. Oh, Mum. Thank you."

"You must say thank you to Eric when you see him after school, Rosie. He bought you the pyjamas and chocolates."

"I will. When can I try out the skates? Can I take them to the park?"

And so it was that on the Friday of Rosie's tenth birthday, her mother said if the weather stayed fine they could take their lunch into Myrtle Park and try out the roller boots for the first time.

At the kiosk in the park Jenny had taken delivery of canned drinks and had just boiled up the small kettle to make a cup of tea for herself. The forecast for the day was excellent. She'd already wound down the awning. A high, June sun was beating down on the kiosk and people were in short sleeves and summer dresses. The flower beds surrounding the bowling green and beside the kiosk were full of colour. Blue delphiniums stood tall as church spires behind swathes of lower growing summer blooms. On the crown green matches were in full swing, the teams wearing whites and sun hats. There was the sound of polite applause from surrounding benches filled with mothers and babes and older folk enjoying the entertainment in the sun and the chance to take the weight off hot feet.

Nobody else would want tea. There was no point in switching on the urn; there'd be a run on cold drinks instead. She dumped her teabag in the waste bin. *Funny, she thought, but even on the hottest days I still like my cup of tea.* A shadow at the window darkened the small space: John.

"Hello, John, lovey," she said. "And what can we do for you today? Forgotten your drink again? There's plenty of choice for you today, love. We've just had in a new delivery."

"No, I didn't forget, thank you. It's just that I've already drunk it. It's hot today. I'm feeling the heat, Jenny. Feeling the heat. I need another drink."

He leaned against the window and ran his hand across his brow as if he were mopping it. He must have seen somebody make that gesture and was copying it, but without a handkerchief.

"What'll it be then?"

"Fizzy lemonade, please."

Jenny pulled a face. "Is fizzy a good idea, lovey?" she said "Haven't you thought you might be better off with a bottle of water? I'd top it up for you here if you wanted."

"What do you mean, top it up? It doesn't need a top. It's already got one."

"Fill it back up again." His face crumpled. "From the tap, John," she explained. "Tap water. Adam's ale. Corporation pop."

"Adam's ale? Corporation pop?"

Give me patience, she thought but didn't say it.

"It's just a saying," she said instead. "You've made a good job in that border by the bowling green, John. That's a lovely display. Beautiful colours."

He stretched his neck and jutted out his chin and seemed to grow even taller with pride.

"Thank you, Jenny," he said. "I asked Chief if I could make a few changes to the plan. I've been learning about colours. It's something called compli - compli- complementary colours. They're the ones that look good together. Did you know that blue and yellow don't always make green?"

"I thought that was exactly how you make green."

"It depends on which yellow and which blue you use. There are cold colours and warm colours and you could end up with a muddy colour if you're not careful."

"Well, I never."

"Never what?"

"Never knew that, John," she said.

"You know now. I'll have two bottles of water, please."

She brought them from the fridge and he went away with them. Jenny could tell he was pleased with himself. He had an odd way of walking when he was feeling self-satisfied. He set off with a little skip and raised himself up onto his toes with an accompanying dip of the head for his first few steps. She watched him prance away and out of sight. She knew it wouldn't be long before she heard him find a way to use the words *Adam's ale*.

The usual midday rush was beginning to thin out. As she'd expected, cold drinks and ice creams had been the order of the day. Her legs ached with all the dashing about she'd had to do since Donna had suddenly quit her part time job. She'd found something with better pay. Couldn't blame her really. The kiosk position hadn't been advertised. The council must be saving money wherever they could. It seemed they expected Jenny to do everything herself. Her customers hadn't minded the delay, though. They were a gentle lot, on the whole, the people who frequented the park at lunchtimes: pensioners in the main, used to taking things slowly. They'd waited patiently. In fact, some hadn't even noticed the queue was longer than usual and they'd had to wait longer to be served. Most of them knew each other anyway, had struck up conversations and shuffled forwards in line without batting an eye.

The lady who worked on the cash out at the supermarket had been with her daughter. The child, Rosie was having her birthday and it was obvious how happy the girl was with her birthday present. She'd babbled on about her new roller boots and gone into great lengths to explain to Jenny how she wanted to learn going backwards. She was practising out on the path now, on the flat area near the animal enclosures.

In Myrtle Park, in the middle of June, it was quite possible to forget you were in Kingsley. When you really looked at John's flower beds, the great variety of trees and the grand sweep of grassland that ran all the way down to the river, it made you forget that in surrounding streets there might be real hardship, poverty even. There were people who truly could not afford to buy ice creams for their children without having to go short on something else. Everything was such a price these days, especially since decimalisation; it was a wonder how some of them managed to keep their heads up. But they did. They brought their own picnic lunches into the park so they didn't need to buy anything and, somehow, their children seemed to know not to ask for something from the shop.

The sound of people running broke her from her thoughts. A crowd was rushing past the little kiosk window. She could hear shouting and the high-pitched wail of a child screaming.

Chapter Eight

John was up by the park wall busily sorting compostables from plastic rubbish and recyclable tin cans which he would then bag up for the waste collection. There was a lot of bending up and down and he was glad of the bank of mature beech trees running alongside the wall which provided shade while he worked. The June mini-heatwave had had him *feeling the heat* and it didn't help wearing the overalls he was obliged to use. The chief gardener had suggested to him he might like to come to work in shorts. He would still have to put the overalls on top but it ought to be better than the heavy denim jeans he usually wore. John had refused. He'd heard enough comments about his *spider legs* to last him a lifetime. Walking from his home to get to work with his legs on show was the last thing he wanted to do even if it was only a short distance.

He straightened up and stretched. His mouth felt dry. He needed a drink but his bottle of water was in the work hut behind the rabbit and budgie enclosures. He tied up the top of a full bag of recyclables and leaned it up against the wall before making his way there.

He'd thought the work hut would be the best place to keep his drink but it turned out it was even hotter than outside. He wondered whether the chief might consider getting them a small fridge to put in the corner under the counter top. They had an electricity supply for the old radio the chief sometimes had on and John knew you could get a small fridge for not much money at all from one of the charity or second hand shops in town.

The hut door banged open behind him. Hot air rushed around his head. There was a scuffling noise and he stumbled as a thick body pressed him up against the bench. He disliked the sensation of someone else's body so close and wanted to wriggle away but a large hand gripped the back of his neck and forced his head forward.

"Playing with yourself are ya, Spazza?" a voice sneered right up against his ear.

John recognised the voice. He concentrated on staying calm. "I'm just going to get a drink of water," he managed to say.

"He's wanked himself stupid," another voice said and then two voices laughed.

"Nah, he's always been stupid," the first voice said and then both laughed again.

"I know what that word means," John said. "And I haven't been doing that. That's a very private thing and you shouldn't talk about it. I know the difference between private things and things you can do in public. I do know what is appropriate behaviour."

The hand on his neck squeezed harder. "Have you heard this? I *do* know what is appropriate behaviour. Who taught you to talk like that? He's a nutcase," the voice said.

"I told you, I want to get a drink."

"Give him his drink, Nick," the first voice said. "I bet it's in his little kiddies' backpack over there."

John heard the sound of a zip fastener. He knew they'd found the pocket where he'd put his bottle of water. The hand forced his head further down and one of the intruders emptied the bottle's contents on his head. Water ran inside the collar of his overalls and right down the back of his neck.

"It's all right," he said. "Jenny will top it up for me."

"He's nuts, Baz. Absolutely fucking nuts. Look at him. The idiot's still smiling."

The grip released his neck and John straightened up. He turned around in time to see the two bullies disappear through the door, laughing at their joke, enjoying what they'd done.

John brushed back his hair with his hand and tried to straighten his collar. He bent down to pick up his backpack where they'd thrown it on the floor. He reached into the inner pocket and brought out a second bottle of water the bullies hadn't found. He smiled. So who was stupid now?

John knew who they were. Baz and Nick had singled him out for their callous treatment since his days on the school bus when he used to count the colours on front doors in the council estate. So he knew how to handle it now. He closed his eyes and did his breathing. His social worker, Andy Bishop had helped him learn how to do it. Just like when he'd count *coral, green, shitty yellow, blue,* he breathed in and out slowly and with all the control he could manage until the ache inside him began to subside. He decided to tell Andy how much his advice had helped when they had their next meeting.

A scream from outside shattered his thoughts. It came from nearby. Somebody needed help. Had those two monsters hurt somebody else? Water bottle in hand, he raced out the door and followed the noise. There, by the rabbits' enclosure lay the little girl who liked his favourite bench. She had on some roller boots and it looked like she'd fallen. There was a nasty graze down the side of her leg and blood was coming out of it. He rushed to her side and scooped her up. Then he ran with her to the corporation green bench because if it made his sandwiches taste better it might make her leg better too.

He settled her in the comfortable "S" shape of his favourite bench and she stopped crying. Gently, he removed the roller boots. The cut on her leg looked dirty with bits of gravel in it. You had to clean cuts like that. Chief had shown him how. He poured water from his bottle on the girl's leg and she howled again, and even though he didn't like touching other people he took out his clean handkerchief and wrapped it around the wound.

"Lie still," he told her. "Somebody will come soon."

He sat beside her and told her everything was going to be all right.

"Rosie! Rosie!" a voice called out. "Are you all right?"

John stood up and the lady he'd seen before ran towards them, sat on the edge of the bench and began fussing over the girl. The girl, Rosie, was sitting up now and making less noise.

"It's really stinging, Mum," she said.

"We need to get you home."

"I'll carry her if you like," John said.

The lady ignored him and said, "Can you stand up, Rosie, do you think?"

Rosie tried. John watched and waited but he knew she was scared to put weight on her leg in case it made it hurt more when she bent or stretched her knee. He raised his eyebrows like you do when you're asking a silent question and the girl said,

"John will carry me home, won't you?"

Chapter Nine

Bending over a small shrub in his front garden, clipping busily at straggling branches of a Berberis that was encroaching on the path, Eric was concentrating on his work when out of the corner of his eye he noticed John rushing into Emerald Street from the direction of Myrtle Park. He was carrying Rosie in his arms and Linda was hurrying alongside. Eric stopped working and stood up straight.

"Good Lord," he said and threw down his clippers. "Linda? John? What's happened?"

"Rosie's had a fall," Linda said, sounding breathless and worried.

"She's hurt her leg, Mr Eric," John added.

"Is it bad? Has she broken anything?" Eric rushed through the gate out into the street to see.

"I think it's just a bad graze, Eric," Linda said.

"Even so. You can never tell. She might need it seeing to."

"Oh, I don't think so. I just need to get her home. This way," she said to John. "We'll go in the front way. It'll be easier carrying her in than through the narrow back alley."

She hurried on along the street carrying Rosie's roller boots while John held Rosie tight.

Eric picked up his clippers and went indoors. He walked through the house and out into the rear yard where he hung them up on a hook in the outhouse. He went back into his kitchen intending to put on the kettle and make himself a cup of tea but he couldn't settle. Slowly, he walked to the front door and stood for a moment. He didn't want to be seen as interfering but he needed to know. He closed the door behind him and picked up pace along the street to number seventeen. He knocked on the door and waited. Linda answered.

Eric said, "I know you'll think I'm sticking my nose in, Linda but I just . ."

"Come in, Eric," she said. "Cup of tea?"

"Where is she?" Eric said as he took a chair at Linda's table.

"She's in the front, on the sofa with her leg up. John's in there with her."

"Ah, it seems he's been quite the hero, hasn't he?"

"Yes. I'm very grateful for his help. I hope he doesn't get into trouble for leaving his work."

"I shouldn't think so. I'll have a word with Harry. He's in charge of the gardens. Known him for years. There won't be any bother. I can pop up there later to explain."

"Speaking of trouble at work," Linda said, "I'd better call in and let them know what's happening."

John suddenly appeared in the doorway. He stepped into the kitchen and pressed his back against the wall. His eyes were staring and he stood rigid, looking troubled.

"Excuse me," he said. "I think she's going to be sick. She's making queer noises and she's gone a funny colour."

Linda grabbed the empty washing up bowl and a tea towel and rushed away. Eric could hear the child coughing and vomiting and Linda telling her daughter it was okay.

"Don't worry, John," Eric said. "It's quite normal. She's had a shock."

"Eric?" Linda called from the living room, "would you come and help us please?"

John stood aside to let Eric pass. "I'll stay here," he said. "I don't like it when people are sick."

Linda was on her knees beside the sofa where Rosie was bending forward quietly sobbing. Eric dropped to his knees alongside.

"My goodness," he said to Rosie. "You're not feeling very well at all, are you sweetheart?"

He reached out to touch her forehead which was clammy and cold. Poor Rosie was a ghastly colour. He took a good look at her injured leg. Silently, he pointed to the swelling around Rosie's ankle and the lurid bruising that had appeared. He looked into Linda's eyes and shook his head.

"Mum, it really hurts," Rosie said. "Not on my leg where it's been bleeding. On my foot."

Eric said, "Can you wiggle your toes, Rosie?"

She couldn't. She said it hurt too much.

"Don't you fret, Rosie. Just you rest there a minute and we'll sort this out. Can you get me a flannel, Linda and run it under the cold tap?"

Linda ran upstairs to fetch one.

Rosie had started shivering. "I don't want a cold flannel on me, Eric," she said. "I already feel cold."

"The cold flannel is for your ankle, Rosie. It'll help."

"Oh, no. Oh, please no. I don't want you to touch it."

"All right. I won't touch you. Just you wait there." He got up and went to meet Linda as she came along the hall carrying the flannel and a pillow. "Linda," he whispered so Rosie wouldn't hear. "I think her ankle is broken but she'll need an X-Ray to be sure. I think we should ring for an ambulance."

Linda brought her hand to her mouth and gasped.

"Now then," Eric said. "Don't take on. There's nothing to worry about. I know Rosie well enough to know she won't be frightened. She'll probably think it's quite an adventure riding in an ambulance."

Linda smiled and nodded but she still looked anxious. "Yes, you're right," she said. "I do tend to panic a bit. Thank you so much just for being here, Eric."

"When the ambulance comes you lock up and go with her. I'll take John up to mine. We'll have a bite to eat and then I'll go with him to the park to explain why he's been missing."

Linda made the call to emergencies from the phone on the hall stand by the front door. They said they could be there in fifteen minutes. Eric waited while she quickly made a second call to the office at her workplace to explain her absence and a third message to Rosie's school.

"Linda, try not to look so worried when you tell Rosie what's happening," he said as soon as she replaced the receiver.

"Do I?" she said. "Is it so obvious? I've never been much good in an emergency. I always used to rely on . . ."

"Your husband. Yes, I know, love. It's hard when you're on your own. I know how you feel. I'll help you wherever I can."

"Rosie," Linda said as they went into the living room. "Eric thinks we need to let a doctor look at your ankle and so do I."

"Is it broken?" Rosie said.

"It does look as if it is. There's an ambulance on its way. We're going to the hospital so you can have an X-Ray."

"Will it hurt?"

Eric interrupted. "Let's put this cold flannel on where it's hurting now and I know it will help. Linda, have you anything she can take for the pain?"

Linda dashed upstairs again and returned with a small packet Eric recognised.

"Perfect," he said. "Snap one in half for her, will you? And don't forget to tell the ambulance crew what she's taken."

By the time the ambulance arrived Rosie was able to lean on her mother and hop to the door. Eric stood on the pavement beside John as the crew lifted Rosie into a wheelchair in the back of the ambulance and her mother climbed in behind her.

"Eric? Can't we go too?" John said.

"There's no need for all of us. We don't want to get in the way, do we?"

"But what if Rosie needs me to carry her again?"

"You can help again when they get back. They won't be long. Come on, let's go on up to my house," Eric said and threw a comforting arm around John's shoulders as they moved off along Emerald Street.

In Eric's kitchen John sat with a drink and a fried egg sandwich while Eric explained the usual procedure for treating broken bones. John wasn't really listening. He was thinking what a strange day it was turning out to be. He'd been inside two people's homes, one after the other, strange surroundings with things in different places from where he kept his own belongings. He looked at everything: the curtains, the floor covering, the furniture. He liked to place himself firmly within a room, to feel himself in it in the picture he built in his mind so that he knew he belonged there and was safe. That was easy to do when he was at home in his own place. It had been a very long time since he'd stepped inside someone else's house.

Yet he didn't feel uncomfortable. He had coped. He hadn't needed to do his special breathing exercises. It must have been because there was something happening more important than how he was feeling. The thought made him smile. Here he was, he told himself, sitting in Mr Eric's kitchen eating a lovely sandwich and talking about what they were going to do about helping Rosie when she came back from the hospital. When they'd chatted together in Myrtle Park all they'd ever talked about before was gardens and plants and how to look after them. It would be nice in future to have something else to talk about when they sat together on his bench. He supposed that was what happened when you had more friends in your life. It meant you would have more things to talk about.

Eric noticed John didn't seem to want to listen to the answers to his questions about broken bones. In fact, at one point he'd looked decidedly squeamish. Then he'd gone into a kind of daze as if he was trying to shut out what he was telling him. Eric changed the subject matter.

"You did absolutely the right thing, John," he said, "taking off Rosie's skating boots for her. Well done. How did you know to do that?"

"I didn't know it was the right thing to do," John said. "I just thought they might feel too heavy if her leg was hurting."

"That was good thinking. And another thing," Eric added. "It was very thoughtful of you to offer to help bring her home. Very kind."

"I like to be kind because I know how it feels when people are not kind."

Eric wasn't sure how to respond but he could imagine well enough how often John must have been the target of others' cruelty. He reached out and rubbed John's shoulder. John flinched.

"I'm sorry, John. I didn't mean to startle you like that. I'll tell you what we'll do," Eric said. "How about when we've finished here I go with you to the park and have a word with Harry? I could let him know why you've been missing from work. I can be there to back you up so he knows you're not making up excuses."

"He knows I always tell the truth. And another thing," John said, imitating Eric's earlier phrase, "I call him Chief."

"Do you?"

"Yes. I think he likes it better than if I say his real name. He says it sounds more professional."

"I stand corrected," Eric said, feeling admonished but he couldn't help a wry smile.

They finished their lunch and, after they cleared away with John helping to dry the plates and put them away, they walked to the park to look for Harry the Chief gardener. They found him having his own lunch in the work shed. Eric recounted the story of Rosie's fall and broken ankle. Harry said John could take the rest of the day off. John wanted to go back to Emerald Street.

"Eric, would it be okay if I come back with you?" John said. "I want to see if Rosie is feeling better when she comes back from the hospital."

Eric agreed. "Of course you can," he said. "I'll be glad of your company, young feller."

They didn't have to wait long for news. They'd only just left the park and turned into Emerald Street when a taxi pulled up beside them and the driver wound down the window.

"Is your name Eric?" the taxi driver called out. "I've got a young lady in the back here says she knows you."

Rosie waved at them from the back seat of the cab. She was smiling and had colour back in her face. Linda opened the rear passenger window and leaned across.

"John," she said. "Would you help Rosie into the house please?"

The taxi moved off along the street and John ran on ahead. Eric caught up in time to see him lifting Rosie into number seventeen. Her leg was bandaged. Linda was waiting on her doorstep and invited him in.

"Only a dressing?" Eric said, as he went inside. "Is it not broken?"

"Oh, yes it's broken. It's what they called a greenstick fracture," Linda said. "We've to go back on Monday when they say the swelling should have gone down. They'll put on a plaster cast and then she's to keep off her feet as much as possible for two weeks."

"Ouch," Eric said. "That isn't going to be easy for her, is it? Then what?"

"They'll give her a rocker to support the cast for another four weeks."

"I see. Will she be able to go to school with this rocker on her foot?"

"I don't know yet, Eric. There aren't many weeks left until the end of the summer term. We'll have to wait and see."

"She can always come and stay with me while you're at work, Linda," Eric said. "Don't you be worried about that."

Linda and Eric sat together in her kitchen with mugs of tea. In the living room John was watching television with Rosie whose bandaged dressing John was admiring. He hadn't left her side.

"I feel a bit sleepy, John," Rosie said.

"Do you want me to fetch your mum?"

"No. I don't think so. I think I'll just stay here and close my eyes."

"That's what shock does to you," John said. "I learned that at school. If you burn yourself or fall over like you did and hurt yourself, the shock comes afterwards and makes you go to sleep. It happened to me once."

"Did it? What happened?"

John began his explanation but he could see her eyes were droopy, her eyelids heavy and closing slowly as he spoke. He lowered his voice and carried on quietly. When Rosie's mother came in to investigate the quietness, he brought his forefinger to his mouth and shushed. Softly, he got up from the sofa and followed Rosie's mother into her kitchen.

"Is she sleeping?" Eric asked as John took the chair Linda offered.

"Yes. It's what shock can do. I'd like to wait till she wakes up before I go home if that's all right with you, Rosie's mum."

"You can call me Linda," she said. "Would you like a biscuit, John?"

"Yes, please Mrs Linda. I like chocolate ones best," he said.

Linda watched him enjoy two chocolate digestives. He had a smile on his face that spread to his eyes. He was like a child, no more advanced in his development than her daughter. But he was such a caring soul. She recalled how carefully he'd held Rosie and carried her all the way from the park to Emerald Street. He was like a big brother to her child. An awkward kind of big brother. Linda wanted to trust him. She wanted to believe Eric when he'd said John wouldn't hurt a fly. The expression on John's face told her he was truly an innocent. But his body? He was a man. Surely he had a man's feelings? Longings. Desires? The two aspects were difficult to reconcile. And yet, here he was, munching on chocolate biscuits and asking to stay until he knew Rosie was feeling better.

She looked into Eric's eyes. He nodded at her as though he understood her unspoken question. She took a chance.

"I've been thinking," she said. "Would you like to come tomorrow for a meal with us, John? I'm sure Rosie would like that. And you'd like to see her again, wouldn't you?"

"I can't come till the afternoon," John said, not looking up from his plate of biscuits. "I help Mrs Midgeley on Saturday mornings. We do the shopping for the old folk who can't get out to do it themselves."

John looked up and straight into her eyes. He grinned across the table at her and she could hardly help the confusing glow inside her at the guilelessness of his expression. Still, she kept her mouth tight shut just in case.

Chapter Ten

Rosie's leg was stiff next day. Stiff and tight. Her mother had removed the dressing over the graze on her leg, applied cream they'd given her at the hospital and left the wound open to the air for a short time as she'd been advised. Her ankle was still swollen and the bruising had spread upwards onto her leg in bands of purple and a sickly green. Rosie rather missed the bandage dressing but John was coming for his tea and it made her happy to know that, at least for one night, he wouldn't be lonely.

He arrived punctually and her mother made a bit of a fuss of him, welcoming him warmly. Rosie balanced on her good leg and leaned on the wall to show him where to hang his coat. She watched as he took pains to hang it perfectly correctly without disturbing the other coats hanging there in the hallway. He smoothed down the sleeves of coats either side of his own before taking off his shoes. In his socks he padded behind her into the living room and sat in the chair facing the television.

"What's on?" he said.

"What do you want to watch?"

"Don't really mind," he said. "What do you usually watch?"

"I don't. Not on Saturdays. I put it on for you."

"I don't usually watch on Saturdays either. After I've helped Mrs Midgeley do the shopping I do my learning."

"What learning?"

"About plants. There's such a lot to learn, you could go on learning forever. I'll never know all there is to know about plants. What do you like to learn about?"

"Well," she said. "I have to do what they tell me at school. So on Saturday afternoons I do that. But there is something I'd like to know how to do."

"What?"

She lowered her voice and whispered, "Magic."

"My mum used to say there's no such thing as magic."

"Well, I think it all depends what kind of magic you're talking about. I know you can't wiggle your nose like the lady on the television programme and make magic happen. But there are things you can do that are a bit like magic."

"What things?"

The living room door swung open and Eric came in.

"Your mother's putting out the food now, Rosie," he said. "What were you talking about just now?"

"I was just saying that I'd like to know how to put magic into people's lives," she said.

"Ah," he said with a knowing nod. "Kind deeds can do that, Rosie."

John wanted to know *exactly* which kind deeds Eric meant.

"Like you did yesterday, John. You helped Rosie home. You knew what to do. But sometimes you have to put some extra thought into it."

Eric tried to explain that different people appreciated different things so you had to know what kind of things people liked first.

Rosie said, "You mean, like you wouldn't give chocolates to someone who wasn't allowed to have them?"

"Something like that, yes."

"Or a book about cooking to someone who likes plants," John added.

"But they might like cooking *and* plants," Rosie said. "How can you tell what people like until you get to know them better?"

Linda called them to the table and the conversation stopped for a while. John thanked her for his plate and wasted no time starting. Rosie could see how much John was enjoying her mother's cooking. The shared dinner was a comforting experience. It felt almost like they were all a real family. Rosie knew she had a smile on her face the whole time as she looked around the table at her mother, John and honorary grandfather, Eric who had on a new shirt. You could tell it was brand new because it still had creases on it from the packaging. John was wearing a tee shirt with his jeans but he was all clean and smart, not like in the park when he sometimes was covered in dirty smudges. Rosie wiggled her nose like on the television show because it was already beginning to feel like magic was happening.

Then, Eric must have still been thinking about kind deeds because he laid down his fork and said,

"It was very kind of you, John, to help Rosie yesterday. Kindness is very important."

"Yes, I know," John said. "People who are not kind are horrible people."

Rosie said, "But it's easier to be kind to people you know, isn't it? I mean, I think it must be harder to be kind to strangers."

Eric said, "Hmm," and thought for a minute. "In the nineteen fifties I once found a book somebody had left behind on the train from Bradford."

"Did you take it home?" John said. "Wouldn't that be stealing?"

"It wasn't stealing, John. Somebody had forgotten they'd put it down on the seat."

"So what did you do?"

"I handed it in at the ticket office."

Rosie said, "Didn't you want to read it first?"

Eric laughed. "Not really," he said. "I looked at the first page and saw it was a special kind of book. It looked very expensive. There were a lot of full colour, glossy illustrated pages of famous works of art. It had a label inside the front page from the art college library. I knew someone would be worried about losing it."

"You could have taken it to the police station," Rosie said.

"I thought the railway ticket office was the best place. The person would realise the last time they had the book in their hands was when they were on the train so that's where they'd go back to look for it."

"But you don't know where they got off," Rosie said.

"Rosie likes to get right to the bottom of everything, Eric," Linda said and popped her eyebrows.

"And I hope you never lose that wonderful curiosity, Rosie. You too, John," Eric said.

John looked pleased Eric had included him and said, "Did the book find its way home?"

"Yes, it did. The next time I was at the station there was a note for me on the ticket office window. I still have it."

"What does it say?"

"If I remember correctly, it says, *'To whoever handed in my 'A History of Art', I can't thank you enough. I may owe my future career to you. I hope I don't let you down.'* Then the young man signed it *David B* and put a coloured drawing of a train on it with a book flying out of the window."

Rosie said, "Who is David B? Is he somebody famous?"

"I can't be sure but there is an artist called David Blakeney," Eric said. "When he was a young man he was a student at the art college in Bradford before he went to London. Now he's super famous in America. Everybody there knows his name. The book might have been his."

"Oh," Rosie said. "That's a lovely story. By being kind you might have made magic happen in *his* life."

"Getting his book back must have made it happen," John added.

Rosie sighed and said,"Wouldn't it be fantastic if we could do something like that?"

"Rosie, eat your tea," Linda said and the conversation stopped.

"Is there some pudding?" John said. "My mum always made puddings at the weekend."

"Yes, John, there is. It's chocolate."

John cleared his plate quickly and sat with the broadest grin on his face waiting for his chocolate pudding. Afterwards, he insisted on helping with washing up because that was good manners, he said, and because it was always important to show new friends you knew how to behave.

Eric joined Rosie and John in the living room while Linda finished tidying in the kitchen.

"Eric, I liked your story about the book on the train," Rosie said.

John nodded his agreement and said, "We could do something like that."

"You mean give people a book to read?"

"Yes, why not?" Eric said. "That's a good idea, John. You could leave a book somewhere for people to find."

Rosie liked the sound of that. "Where could we leave it?" she said.

"Oh, in a bus stop or . . . on a park bench."

Rosie's eyes lit up and she leapt from the sofa. She hopped around the room in a burst of energy, her injured leg held out in front.

"That's what we're going to do, John," she said and quickly sat down again. "We're going to choose a book to leave on our favourite bench in the park for other people to read. You'll be able to keep an eye on it when you're at work."

"I've got a book I've never read," John said. "My mum got it for me when I was little. You could use that."

"What is it?"

"It's called *Treasure Island*."

"What's it about?"

"I don't know. I told you, I've never read it myself. Mum used to read some of it to me, so I know there's somebody in it called Long John. But that's all I remember."

"It's about pirates and the search for hidden treasure," Eric told them. "I read it myself when I was a boy."

"And do the pirates find the treasure?" Rosie said.

"Oh, that would be telling. You'll have to read it for yourself. Why don't you make some arrangements between you? Let me know what you decide and I'll help you, if you like. I wouldn't mind reading it again. I'll leave that thought with you," he said and went back to the kitchen.

"We're going to make it work, John," Rosie said when they were on their own again. "We're going to make magic. I've noticed when my mum is reading a book from the library she always gets a kind of smile on her face. Well, no, sometimes she doesn't. Sometimes she gets tears in her eyes."

"From reading a book?" John said. "I wouldn't want to read a book that made people cry."

"I think some people must like that, mustn't they? Or else they wouldn't choose books like that. But mostly Mum smiles when she's reading. Just think, that's what we're going to do. Put smiles on people's faces. That's like magic, isn't it?"

John wasn't sure. "I suppose so," he said. "But what if they don't bring the book back?"

"They will. I'll make a note to put inside and then they'll know they have to bring it back to the bench so the magic can spread to other people."

"Are we going to use my book?"

"Yes. But first we're going to read it."

John groaned and screwed up his nose. "I had problems when I tried."

"Don't worry. We'll do it together. You have to bring it here so we can get some help. Eric said he would. My mum might too."

The god of putting things right must have been listening. Something fired his interest and he recognised an opportunity. He couldn't resist reaching down from the clouds and stretching out his arm toward Kingsley and number seventeen Emerald Street.

Here was his chance to play without getting too personally involved. He would be able to watch from afar while others did his work for him. It would be another twenty five years or more before the practice and benefits of Book Crossing became known worldwide but the god of putting things right knows that Rosie and John were the first ever when they took their early steps toward the beginning of the Kingsley Treasure Island reading group.

Chapter Eleven

Although John recognised the onset of familiar feelings of anxiety stirring in his stomach that happened whenever there were big changes about to happen in his life, he nevertheless looked forward to reading with Rosie. He had confidence that she wasn't the sort of person to make fun of him about his poor reading skills. She was a kind person. He made up his mind to see it through and do his best.

On Sunday morning he took out the storage box from under his bed where he kept all his treasures and mementoes of his mother. The book was at the bottom of the box, wrapped in the favourite waist apron she always wore when she was cooking Sunday dinner. He brought the apron to his nose and sniffed at it. It didn't smell of his mother any more but he liked the feel of it against his cheek. It was almost like a hug from her. He'd forgotten what loving hugs felt like.

He unwrapped the book, opened it and looked at the first page. There was a map of an island with places named on it but he couldn't decipher most of it because the writing was in old fashioned script. He could make out a place called *Ye Spyeglass Hill* and another called *Skeleton Island* but that was all. He turned the pages to the first chapter.

Even the first paragraph was difficult. He didn't know what a squire was so he skipped to the description of the brown old seaman with a sabre cut across one cheek. He knew a sabre was a sword and carried on reading but when he reached the nut-brown seaman saying, '*This is a handy cove, and a pleasant sittyated grog-shop*' he sighed and realised he could go no further. He hoped Rosie would be able to explain.

After one last sniff of his mother's apron he replaced it in his storage box and slid it back under the bed. He stayed on his knees trying to recall what they'd had to eat the last time she'd cooked for him but the memory was lost. It was a shame, he thought, to lose good memories. If the memory was painful, like the day he learned his mum had died in hospital, it was a good thing to forget the distressing details of it. You didn't have to feel guilty about shutting out the hurtful things. They had already caused a lot of damage. It was okay to stop them from hurting you forever. He decided to stop trying to remember what their last meal together had been. Sometimes you had to let things go or you'd get upset all over again. His social worker, Andy Bishop had helped him learn how you can change your own thoughts to make yourself feel better. You have to concentrate on pushing out the bad thoughts and looking for the good ones.

There were no Sunday special dinners any more and that was bad, but he'd had a nice tea with Rosie and her mum and Mr Eric and he could look forward to his next meeting with Andy and their monthly night out. And, as well as that, there was the first reading of Treasure Island at Rosie's house. Good things were happening and they seemed to be coming all at once. His wall calendar in the kitchen had an exciting number of circled reminders on it.

His efforts at concentration had worked. He pushed himself up onto his feet. He put *Treasure Island* on the small table next to his bed where he would see it in the mornings and not forget to take it with him when he went to Rosie's house on Tuesday after work. He spent the rest of Sunday morning sorting out his laundry and getting his things ready for work. He checked what was on television so he could plan his evening's viewing before he got out the vacuum cleaner. It didn't take long to whizz through the single-storey house as there wasn't much dusty stuff to suck up: he was always careful to take off his outdoor shoes before he came indoors.

He kept his small, galley kitchen as clean as his mother would approve of and always washed up straight after he'd eaten anything, even his cereal bowl first thing in the morning. It was better to come home after a day's work to a smart, tidy kitchen with no jobs left over to do before you could start preparing the next meal. He was proud Mrs Midgeley, the warden always commented on his housekeeping skills whenever she popped in to say hello on her way to check on the elderly residents who couldn't help themselves as much as he could.

"You can come and live with me, John, any time you like," she'd say. "You'd be no trouble at all. I can see that. Look at that shine you've got on the coffee table. You can see your face in it."

Sometimes she'd stay and have a cup of tea with him after they'd done the Saturday morning shopping for the older residents who couldn't do it any more. He knew she didn't really want him to go and live with her. People always did that: say things that sounded nice but never meant to do it. It had taken him a long time to understand that when people said see you later, they didn't mean they were going to come back in a short time, or even today. They meant they'd see you again sometime. It was a saying much like the ones Jenny used all the time. He often thought life would be easier if everybody said what they meant and meant what they said.

He took a walk in the park in the afternoon to check on his flower beds. There would be some dead-heading do to next day so the plants could make more flowers instead of seeds. He walked past the tuck shop and waved at Jenny who was very busy with customers.

"See you tomorrow," he called out to her.

"Right you are," she shouted through the ridiculous serving hatch and waved back.

He popped in at the corner paper shop on his way back. He bought his Sunday bar of chocolate and collected his new favourite comic that he'd only recently discovered: The Incredible Hulk, imported all the way from America.

"I think the Hulk would make an exciting television programme," he said to the shopkeeper, Mr Thompson.

"How would they get the actor to turn green?" Thompson said.

"They can do all kinds of things now," John said. "Did you see Planet of the Apes at the cinema?"

"I see what you mean," Mr Thompson said. "You're right. I expect we will see the Hulk on television one day"

"Thank you," John said as he collected his change. "See you later."

"Mind how you go."

"I will. I'm always careful."

John enjoyed all the super hero comics and, when he grew tired of reading them again, he gave them to Mrs Midgeley for her grandson. He had leftover beef that Mrs Midgeley had roasted for him with a bubble and squeak of leftover vegetables for his evening meal, washed up and settled in his armchair to watch Sunday night at the London Palladium before he went to bed.

Monday was a busy day at work in the park. There was always a lot of litter to clear up and bins to empty after the weekend but John was glad to be occupied. He hoped everything was going to be all right for Rosie when she went back to the hospital about her broken ankle but he didn't want to have to think about it too much. The idea of bones snapping in two made his insides go queer so keeping his mind focused on his work distracted him from unpleasant thoughts. He put extra effort into his sweeping and avoided his favourite corporation green bench at lunchtime in case it brought back memories of bruised and bleeding legs he didn't want to remember. He sat at one of the small tables Jenny had put outside the shop instead.

"Hello, John," Jenny called from the shop doorway. "Everything all right, lovey?"

"Yes thank you," he said as Jenny stepped out and came closer.

"Everything all right with the girl who fell last Friday? Rosie, is it? Harry tells me you helped take her home."

"Yes I did. She broke her ankle."

"Oh no! Oh, dear. And she was so thrilled to have those new roller boots. Fancy, on her birthday as well. What a carry on. She'll have a pot on it, no doubt."

John didn't know what she meant.

"What's a pot?" he said.

"It's what they put on broken bones to hold them in place while they heal. It's like a big bandage that they wet and as it dries it goes hard."

"So why is it called a pot?"

"Well, I suppose because of what it looks like. It goes hard and white when it dries and looks like what a pottery plate is made of."

"That must be heavy," John said. "I don't think I'd like one on me."

He got up to put his rubbish in the bin. "Are these tables out here new?" he said, wanting to move the subject away from broken bones.

"That they are, lovey. I've just had them delivered this morning. Don't they make the place look pretty? It looks like somewhere on the continent now, don't you think?" she said gazing over the circular tables and folding chairs. "You could imagine you were in Paris or somewhere in Switzerland."

"I've got to go now, Jenny. Chief wants me to check in the play area. I have to look all round the area and under the swings for dog shit."

John could hear Jenny tutting as she went back inside.

On Monday evening Andy Bishop, John's social worker and supporter was coming to pick him up for their monthly catch up. John always enjoyed his evenings out with Andy. He liked riding in Andy's car too, even though it was too low to see over people's garden walls to practise identifying plants in their gardens. He didn't know for sure how old Andy was and would never ask. He thought it was rude to ask outright but he guessed Andy must be older than himself to have such an important job.

He had a lot to thank Andy for. He'd shown him how to shave properly, what best to use to scrape the hairs away and how to take proper care of his shaving kit. He reckoned that was the sort of thing fathers would tell their sons. But John had never had a father to show him how to do things. He'd just had Andy. Since John's teenage years there'd only been Andy to help him. That made him a father figure, John supposed, and it was fairly easy to think of him that way. Andy wasn't as tall as himself and his hair was a lighter colour. He sometimes came in his walking shorts on summer evenings so John knew he didn't have hairy legs either. What he did have was a kind of calm way of explaining things that made you have confidence in him. He spoke quietly and never sounded bossy.

Andy arrived at his usual time.

"Hi, John, ready to go?" Andy said.

"I'm always ready on time."

"Ah, but I might catch you out one day."

"No, you won't."

They both laughed and John clambered in to the front passenger seat. They went for burgers and sat indoors to eat because it looked as if it was going to rain.

"I have a new friend," John said as soon as they were settled. "Her name is Rosie. Her mum is a friend too. I've been to their house. And Eric's."

"That's a lot of new friends, John," Andy said. "What can you tell me about them?"

"Rosie fell in the park and hurt her leg. I helped her to get home."

"That was a kind thing to do, John. Good for you. Did you know Rosie before?"

"Before what?"

"Before she fell."

"Yes. Rosie and her mum, Mrs Linda have their lunch break in the park sometimes. They used to sit on my favourite bench. I didn't like it at first but now it's all right. I don't mind sharing now."

"Because you know them?"

"Yes. I had tea at their house on Saturday. Eric was there too."

"Eric?"

"Yes. He might be Rosie's granddad. I don't know. I didn't ask."

"How old is Rosie, John?"

"I don't know that either. I know she had a birthday. That's why she had on roller skate things. She was learning how to do it."

"But then she had a fall?"

"Yes. That's how it happened."

"And you helped her to get home. Was her mother there with you?"

"Yes. She let me pick Rosie up and carry her all the way to their house."

"Was that far to go?"

"Not really. Emerald Street. Number seventeen. I made sure to remember it. And Eric lives at the house at the end of the street but I don't know the number yet."

"So, how's things at Myrtle park?" Andy asked. "Did you get a fridge in your work hut?"

"Not yet."

"Otherwise things are all okay?"

"Good," John said, taking a bite from his burger. "Pretty much the same as always but good. Except for the bullies."

"What bullies?"

"It doesn't matter."

"Don't you want to tell me about it? I might be able to help."

John stopped chewing and put down his food. "It's some boys I remember from when I went to school," he said. "They stole my bottle of water and poured it over me, but it didn't matter because I had another one. Is there any more sauce?"

Andy passed him another small pot of ketchup. "Do you know their names?" he said.

"Not their real names, no. One is called Baz and the other one is Nick. That could be his real name I suppose."

"And they went to the same school as you?"

"No. They got off the bus before me. They went to the school with shitty yellow paint."

"Oh, okay. I know the school you mean. You know, John, there's something I've always wanted to know. Can I ask you something? Why do you call it shitty yellow?"

It was the first time anybody had bothered to ask him. It pleased him the first person was his friend and supporter Andy. John smiled and leaned back in his chair. He folded his arms across his chest and nodded the importance of his response as he spoke.

"I call it shitty yellow because my mum did. Not all yellows are shitty, though. Some yellows are nice like sunshine. I've been learning all about colours. Shitty yellows are the ones that look like what happens in a new baby's nappy."

"I see," Andy said. "I understand now. Thank you for explaining that to me."

John saw that Andy was smiling and his eyes had crinkled up but he wasn't aware he'd said anything funny. He wanted to explain more.

"I like to say things my mum used to say," he said, feeling he needed to make it clear for Andy. "It makes me feel as if she's still here."

"There's nothing wrong with that, John. I think your mother would be very proud of you if she knew what a great job you're doing with the flower beds in the park."

"Yes," John agreed. "I'm good at it. I'm an excellent gardener."

Their conversation paused while they decided on dessert. Andy was the first to speak again.

"About those bullies, Baz and Nick. Leave it with me, John. I'll see what I can do."

John said, "I don't want to cause any trouble."

"You won't cause trouble. They're the ones causing trouble, aren't they? They might be doing it to other people too."

"Oh, I didn't think of that. I wouldn't like that."

"No. Neither would I. People like those two enjoy frightening people. I know you're strong but not everybody is. If we could help them be safe from bullies it would be the right thing to do, wouldn't it?"

"Oh, yes," John said. "I want to help."

Chapter Twelve

On Tuesday evening John arrived at number seventeen Emerald Street with Treasure Island in his backpack. He'd rewrapped it in his mother's apron because that's where it belonged. It didn't feel right for him to leave the apron behind. Reading the book his mother had bought for him was another way to feel that she was still close. She wouldn't be waiting at home for him to tell her all about it when he got back, but he knew he'd hold a special feeling within him that he had done something that would have pleased her.

Linda took him to their living room where Rosie was waiting. When he took the book from his backpack he told Rosie why he'd felt it important to retrieve the apron from the box under his bed and rewrap the book in it.

"That's a lovely thing to do," she said and held out her hands for it. John thought she looked as if she couldn't wait to get her hands on his book.

"We will be careful with it, won't we?" he said.

"Yes, John," Rosie said. "Our plan to make magic happen in other people's lives depends on this book."

She was sitting on the sofa with her injured leg up on a cushion. From below her knee a solid, white plaster cast encased her leg with just the tip of her toes peeping out of the end. John handed her his precious book.

"It looks so old," she said, sliding her fingers across it. "You don't see children's books like this today."

It was true. It was a hardback book with a faded dust sheet bearing a coloured illustration of pirates fighting with swords. On the inside flap the price was marked as 4/-, a strange symbol Rosie recognised but had forgotten the value. Her mother told them it was the old way of calling money pounds, shillings and pence. The symbol priced the book at four shillings.

"I've forgotten. What was a shilling?" Rosie wanted to know.

"Five pence today," Linda said.

"So four shillings would be twenty pence?"

"Yes."

"But you couldn't buy a book like this for twenty pence today, could you, Mum?"

"No, you couldn't."

"Mrs Midgeley where I live says everything has got more expensive since they changed the money," John said.

"She's right, John. I'm not sure how much of that has to do with going decimal, though. I think in some places they've added on a bit extra as well. I'll leave you two to get on shall I? I've a few jobs to do."

"Sit down, John," Rosie said. "Let's get started."

The Tuesday evening first reading of Treasure Island didn't go well. Rosie had to sit still with her leg up on the sofa and couldn't get comfortable. Try as they might, there didn't seem to be a way possible for them both to look at the pages at the same time. John wanted to know how long it would be before she could get up and walk about.

"Two whole weeks," she said. "I have to keep my weight off it and stay still as much as I can but it's boring just sitting here with nothing to do except watch television."

John attempted to comfort her.

"That's why it's a good idea to have a book to read, isn't it?" he said.

Rosie sighed and looked downhearted. "It would be if there weren't so many words in it we have to look up in the dictionary."

"I thought this was supposed to be a book for children," John said looking disappointed.

"It is," Rosie said. "Maybe children knew different words when the book was written from the words we use now. I'd no idea it was going to be so difficult."

"And you're a much better reader than I am," John said. "Imagine how it feels to me, Rosie. I don't stand a chance."

Rosie went quiet for a moment.

"I'm sorry, John," she said. "I've only been thinking about myself. I should have thought more about what I was asking you to do."

"I've got an idea," John said and went to find Rosie's mother.

He found her in the back yard taking down washing from the line. John offered to hold up the basket to save her bending up and down so much.

"Mrs Linda," he said, "I'm sorry but we're stuck. Me and Rosie need some help with my book."

He waited, hoping she would make an offer.

"Give me five minutes," Linda said, "and I'll be with you."

He ran back indoors to tell Rosie the news. Linda wasn't far behind him.

"I've already had a chat with Eric about it," she told them. "We thought you might need a bit of help with the reading. I'll come and read with you now but Eric said he'd like to come and read with you as well. He says he remembers it from when he was a boy but he'd love to read it again."

They set up a reading system, taking turns with chapters and stopping only every now and then to look in a dictionary. On the evening readings when Rosie's mum was with them they'd have chocolate biscuits and milk while they talked about what they'd just read. John couldn't understand why the word *boatswain* was pronounced *bosun* but eventually accepted that very old words still kept their old-fashioned spelling.

When Linda was working a later shift at the supermarket she stopped at Eric's house on her way out to leave the book with him so he could catch up before his turn to read that evening. While Rosie still had to keep off her feet, progress was slow. On some evenings when it was Linda's turn, she apologised for being too tired to read. They had their chocolate biscuits and watched television instead. Then Eric caught a summer cold and couldn't come along to number seventeen to do his evening read.

Rosie didn't go back to school that summer. By the time she had the rocker plate fitted beneath her plaster cast there was very little left of the school term. As soon as she learned how she could walk with the block beneath her foot they had Eric's readings at his house. It was good practice for her, she said, to get used to a different way of walking.

John liked Eric's house. The rooms were the same shape and size as in Rosie's but all the furniture was different. Eric's sofa was bigger and better for his long legs. He could stretch out and feel comfortably relaxed.

But Treasure Island by Robert Louis Stevenson proved to be a difficult read for both John and Rosie. Right from the beginning words such as ' *I take up my pen in the year of grace 17—, and go back to the time when my father kept the Admiral Benbow inn'*, were difficult for him to understand. But, *'the brown old seaman, with the sabre-cut'* and the way *'he came plodding to the inn door, his sea chest following behind him in a hand barrow'* set their imaginations alight. Before long they were captivated by the story especially when Eric gave them a tune to sing the old sea dog's song.

'Fifteen men on a dead man's chest -
Yo-ho-ho, and a bottle of rum!'

It became their greeting and their goodbye to one another each time they met for the evening's read. Rosie would call out, 'Yo-ho-ho'. John responded with 'and a bottle of rum'. They revelled in the names of the characters and imagined themselves aboard the *Hispaniola* with Captain Smollett, Squire Trelawney, Dr Livesey, Hawkins and Silver.

"He's the one I remember," John said. "Silver. Long John Silver. Like me. I think that's why my mum chose the book for me. I'm a long John too," and he hobbled around Eric's living room pretending one of his own long legs was made of wood.

"I have good memories of it too," Eric said. "We read it at school when I was just a boy. In my mind's eye I can still see the teacher who read it to us."

"What's a minezye?" John said.

"It's a memory," Eric told him. "It's when a memory is so clear you can almost see it in front of you."

"Ah. I think I know what you mean. I must have a lot of minezyes," John said, and added, "But only in my head."

"It's a very old story, isn't it?" Rosie said. "My mum told me."

Eric showed them where they could find the date of its first publication printed within the first few pages. The year eighteen eighty three was a very long time ago and Rosie wondered if children in those days would have been able to read it by themselves.

The readings with Eric in charge went well. John loved listening to him. He could do different voices for all the characters so that it was like listening to the radio. John enjoyed learning new words like doubloon but was surprised there were three deaths in the story already by the time they reached the end of part one. Some characters came to such violent ends he thought it was shocking to have all that going on in a children's book. In part two he learned what a figure head on a ship was and that the mail meant it was the horse-drawn coach that people could ride in as well as delivering letters. In part three there were two more murders and the word marooned meant somebody left behind on a deserted island.

Rosie didn't seem to be shocked by the number of people dying in the story. She thought it was funny that of all the things the castaway Ben Gunn said he missed most about his old life in England and dream about, he dreamed about cheese.

"What would you miss eating most, John, if you were marooned?" she asked him.

He thought for a moment. "Chocolate," he said. "Or biscuits. Or a hot chocolate drink."

"Ah, but if you were a pirate you'd probably only ever drink rum," Rosie said.

Both John and Rosie struggled at the beginning of part four where the narrator changes and Doctor Livesey takes up the story. They liked the doctor's way of explaining when it feels like your heart skips a beat when he calls it 'dot and carry one', and although the fight scenes were exciting they were sad it was the faithful Tom Redruth who meets his end.

Part five was full of more fighting and more horrible deaths. As Eric read the scene where the wounded Israel Hands climbs the mast with a dagger in his teeth, dragging his injured leg behind him to get at Jim Hawkins, John's eyes grew wide and his mouth fell open. By the time they reached the point where Hawkins is pinned by the shoulder to the mast John was on the edge of his seat.

He had never enjoyed a book as much as when Eric was reading Treasure Island with Rosie and himself. He concentrated on making new minezyes for him to remember in future. Good memories were the ones to keep forever. Treasure Island was high up on his new list of favourites.

Chapter Thirteen

July was nearly over. In Myrtle Park, John was busy replanting beds after a summer storm had flattened flowers around the bowling green. Chief always kept spares in one of the greenhouses for just such an occasion. Tall, purple-topped verbena had taken a battering from high winds and heavy rain. The ones nearest the retaining wall along the short end of the crown green had been protected from the worst of it but along the more open, long side many had succumbed. It was important to replace them, Chief said, because the long summer school holidays were about to begin and that was the park's busiest time. He wanted everything to look tidy. John wanted to get on with it to put right his colour plan. His pink penstemons just in front of the verbena and the cream-coloured impatiens in front of those needed the contrast of the verbena standing tall behind them. He was determined to do a good job and earn Chief's admiration.

He stood back and assessed his work. Chief came alongside.

"That's looking better, John," he said. "Another job well done."

"Thank you, Chief. I always like to do a good job. I will finish it all today."

"Excellent. There's somebody here to see you, John," Chief said.

"Is there? Who?"

"Eric and young Rosie, over by the tuck shop. I think they've brought a picnic. Why don't you take your lunch break now and join them?"

"I'll need to wash my hands first," John said and dashed off.

Rosie had been able to walk well enough on the rocker plate which was nothing much more than a shaped block of light wood. She wanted to take the book to Myrtle Park. They took it slowly, Rosie linking arms with Eric as it was still strange getting used to a new way of walking without feeling she needed to hop.

The final two chapters of Treasure Island were waiting for them. As they sat around one of Jenny's new tables, John ate his packed lunch listening to the culmination of the adventure story. He wanted to know where Ben Gunn got his salt from for his salted goat meat.

"He's been marooned for three years, Eric," he said, using his newly learned word. "He wouldn't have any salt left."

Rosie said, "The sea's salty. He might have soaked it in that and then let it dry in the sun."

"Good idea, Rosie," Eric said. "I bet that's exactly what he did."

"And another thing," John added. "Captain Flint must be very hungry by now. Nobody has given him anything to eat all the way through the story. We feed the budgies and lovebirds here twice a day. Do parrots eat the same things?"

"I don't know, John," Eric said. "I've never had one. I expect they eat seeds and fruit. Shall we get on with reading the end now."

"Yes, please."

"Of Silver we have heard no more," Eric read.

John sighed, and said, "Good. I'm glad. He told good people bad lies."

Eric continued reading aloud. *"Oxen and wain-ropes would not bring me back again to that accursed island; and the worst dreams that ever I have are when I hear the surf booming about its coasts, or start upright in bed, with the sharp voice of Captain Flint still ringing in my ears: Pieces of eight! Pieces of eight!"*

Jenny came out to see what they were doing. "Pieces of eight?" she said.

"It's what Captain Flint says while he's sitting on Long John's shoulder," John said.

"Excuse me, but I don't know what on earth you're talking about," Jenny said, shaking her head. "Who is sitting on whose shoulder?"

"Captain Flint is Long John Silver's parrot," Rosie said. "There was a real, human Captain Flint as well. He was a buccaneer. Pieces of eight are coins, aren't they, Eric?"

"That's right," Eric said. "They were Spanish coins that could be cut into eight pieces."

"They could cut up coins? When was that?" Jenny said. "I think you'd be in trouble if you tried to do that now."

Eric said, "I think they were first made in the fifteenth century. They were made of silver. There's probably a lot more to it than I'm aware of. You could look it up in the library."

"And is all this kind of thing in the book?"

"It's better than that," Rosie said. "There's fighting and shooting muskets and pistols, and pirates and murders and hidden treasure on an island far across the sea."

"Fighting and murders? Eric? Is this a suitable book for these two?"

"It's considered a classic book for children, Jenny."

"Well, I don't know about that. I'm not sure it's something I would choose for children. But I'm happy to see you doing so well now, Rosie," she said. "When can you have the pot taken off?"

"I'm not sure," Rosie said.

"By the end of next month, I believe," Eric said.

"Dearie me," Jenny said. "That's a long time. I bet you'll be glad to be rid of it. Does it give you much trouble, lovey?"

"Sometimes it makes my skin itch inside but I can't reach in to scratch it," Rosie said.

Jenny said, "Does your mum knit?"

"No. Why?"

"I'll bring you one of my knitting needles for next time you come. You can slide down inside the pot so you can reach where it's itching. You have to be careful, though. You have to be gentle. You mustn't be too rough with it. I tell you what, I'd better have a word with your mum first."

"You'll be seeing a lot more of us from now on," Eric said. "The six week summer school holiday is coming up and Rosie is going to spend more time with me."

"Lovely," Jenny said. "We'll reserve you one of our special tables here, but don't tell anybody else you're bringing your own picnic. You'll get me into trouble. I'm supposed to sell food from here. I'm giving you special dispensation." She picked up Treasure Island and added, "So, this is the book with pirates and fighting and murders?"

"Yes. We're going to make magic with it," John said.

"Are you now?" She popped her eyebrows and looked at Eric. "And what kind of magic is that?"

Eric explained Rosie's plan about leaving the book for people to find. "Well, I never heard anything like it," she said.

"We're going to leave it on John's favourite bench where he can keep an eye on it," Rosie said. "It's for other people to take home and read it. Will you help us, Jenny?" Rosie said.

"Of course I will. I wouldn't want anything to happen to spoil your magic. But, what will you do if it rains? Have you thought about that? I think you could leave it here on one of our new tables where there's some shelter from the awning."

They agreed it was a good idea and set a date for the first time to leave Treasure Island for somebody to find. Rosie said she wanted to write a note to go inside the book explaining what they wanted people to do and why. Jenny suggested they might want the use of a clear plastic box to put the book in and said she'd look out for one that might be suitable.

Everything was beginning to fall into place. The god of putting things right must have been smiling. Rosie certainly was. She could hardly wait to begin the magic. John finished his packed lunch and said he had to get back to work. There were still more Verbenas to plant, he said. Chief expected him to complete the job before the end of the day.

Eric took Rosie to Myrtle Park on the first Friday in August while her mother was at work. Jenny had set aside a table for them so they would be able to watch and see who took Treasure Island for the first time. Eric had helped Rosie with the wording of her note to put inside it and, using some double-sided sellotape he fixed it inside the hard cover of the book. John came to the tuck shop to join them.

The day was warm and pleasant and so was the dry breeze that blew gently through the trees bringing with it the perfume of a jasmine John had recently planted to climb the trellis on the tuck shop wall. The forecast was good. It hadn't been necessary to use the container box Jenny had found. It was an ideal day for magic. Rosie set down the book on the bench and went back to sit at the table. They waited and watched.

Hugo Fairclough was the first taker. Neither Rosie nor John knew who he was. They watched, hardly daring to breathe as the man picked up the book from

John's favourite, corporation green bench. He opened it and sat to read the note inside. Then he looked around and spotted Eric and the others at their table by the kiosk. He got up again and walked toward them bringing the book with him.

"Do you know anything about this?" he said. "Somebody has deliberately left this book on the bench."

"Hugo," Eric said, "this is Rosie who wrote the note inside. It's all her idea. We're just helping."

The man smiled at Rosie and said, "What a wonderful idea. Am I the first to receive the magic? I see there aren't any other notes besides your own."

"Yes, sir," Rosie said. "I hope the god of putting things right knows what to do for you."

"The god of putting things right?" Hugo asked. "I didn't know there was one."

"He's like Tinker Bell," she answered. "You have to believe in him or else the magic won't work."

"I see. Oh, well then. I must be on my best behaviour. Thank you so much, Rosie. I shall do my best. It's been a delight to meet you. Eric, I'll be in touch."

When the man had gone Rosie asked how he and Eric knew one another.

"We used to play football together. A long, long time time ago," Eric said.

"I didn't know you played football," John said. "Was it here in Kingsley?"

"No, John. It wasn't. I haven't always lived here. Hugo and I both went to the same school when we lived in a village up in the Dales. It was the village team."

"And then you both decided to come and live in Kingsley," John said.

"Sort of. I came when I married. Hugo joined the army and came after that."

"And you kept in touch with one another," Rosie added.

"That's right. For many years."

"Did you know he was going to come to the park today?"

"I had a little idea he might," Eric said but would give no further detail.

Rosie was already looking forward to the day the book came back. She especially wanted to see if Mr Hugo Fairclough had written his own note to leave behind, but the days passed and there was no sign of him coming back to the park to return it.

The following Friday Eric had a doctor's appointment so, with Linda's agreement, Rosie was to stay with Jenny at the tuck shop until he came back. She found it was fun helping out with Jenny. Rosie's job was to clear the outside tables when people had finished and wipe the cloth clean. If it was windy she was to make sure the cloths were fastened securely by the special hooks that clipped them to the table tops or else they'd blow away. Also, it was her job to make sure all litter went in the bin. There was washing up to do, and more clearing away and more washing up. She was glad of the awning providing cool shade. The day was hot and hobbling about on the rocker plate made her leg ache.

She had just sat down with an ice cream when she saw an elderly gentleman she recognised coming toward her. Hugo Fairclough was bringing Treasure Island back. She noticed straight away he'd put the book in a clear plastic cover. He came to her table and sat.

"Hello, Mr Fairclough," she said.

"Hello Rosie," he said and handed her the book. "I must apologise to you and your friends for keeping it so long. I've written a note and put it inside as you requested and I hope you don't mind me putting a cover on the book. You can still see the illustration through it and I thought it would help to keep it clean."

"No, I don't mind," Rosie said. "It makes it look like a book from the library. Are you going to stay and wait for Eric?"

"Sorry, I can't stay longer though I would like to. When you see Eric will you tell him I'm going away for a few days with my daughter and grandson but I'll be in touch when I return."

"Yes, I'll make sure to tell him. I won't forget. He had an appointment today but I think he'll be back soon if you'd like to change your mind and wait."

"I can't, dear. Not today. We have a train to catch. I just wanted to make sure you got your book back so you can spread the magic further."

Rosie grinned and said, "Did it happen for you?"

"It was wonderful," he said and his eyes were twinkling. "It's all explained in my note. Eat your ice cream, Rosie. It's beginning to melt."

94

She sucked up a big mouthful before it dripped on her dress. "Thank you for telling me," she said.

"And thank you, young lady. I shall look forward to hearing about the book's travels when I come back."

The magic was beginning. Suddenly her leg didn't ache so much. When Eric returned from his appointment she was anxious to tell him. She handed him Hugo's note,

"Will you read it, Eric, please?" she said. "It's in scratchy handwriting. I can't really tell what it says."

Eric unfolded the paper and put on his reading glasses.

"It says, *Dear Rosie and John, Thank you for lending me your precious book. I'm sorry I've had it so long but I've been reading it to my grandchildren a few chapters at a time. I can't tell you how much we've all enjoyed it. Pure magic. You've made me feel young again. I've taken the liberty of putting it in a wipe-clean cover. I hope you don't mind. Good luck with your idea. Hugo Fairclough.*

Eric took off his glasses and slapped his knees.

"Well, how about that?" he said. "It looks as if your idea is going to be a success."

Chapter Fourteen

The rest of August brought high temperatures and high humidity. In the lower field at Myrtle Park there was not an inch to spare in the children's paddling pool. Toddlers held on to an adult guiding them through the water, almost waist high on the smallest ones. Around the pool, older youngsters were being supervised by parents on deck chairs taken from the supply provided. Throughout the long summer school holidays the little playground was full of children playing on the climbing frames and riding on spinning tables and see-saws. Older children used the higher, bigger swings nearer the tennis courts where teenagers played round robin competitions and argued over calling balls out. The crown bowling green was used every day and every seat on every bench was taken.

At the tuck shop Rosie wanted to see what else there was inside so she'd know where everything was kept and how Jenny kept track of sales and replacement stock. Jenny showed her inside the freezers.

"I never thought to show you, Rosie," Jenny said. "I should have realised you'd like to know how everything works."

"What's behind this door?" Rosie asked.

"Open it if you like."

Rosie knew the ground floor of the lodge had been converted for its present use from the small house it used to be but she was surprised to discover a staircase behind the door in the storage room leading to an upper floor. Jenny said she could go up carefully and followed on behind.

There had been one bedroom up the stairs under a vaulted ceiling but the conversion hadn't gone so far as including electrical wiring up there. There was no power and therefore no lighting or heating.

"What are these things sticking out of the wall?" Rosie said.

"They used to be the lights," Jenny said. "They were called gas mantles."

"Gas? Like on gas cookers and fires?"

"Yes. When this old place was built they didn't have electricity. They would turn the gas on and set it alight. Then they popped these gauzes over the flame."

Rosie said, "But, wouldn't that have been dangerous?"

"Maybe it was. But I suppose people in those days would have been more frightened by electricity, something new to them. They wouldn't understand how it works."

"Those gas lights must be very old, mustn't they?" Rosie said when they went back down.

"Very. I bet they go back as far as Queen Victoria. I don't go up there. There's no need. We keep this door at the bottom closed all the time. Well, now you know where we keep everything. We'd better get back to work."

Sales of ice cream, iced lollipops and chilled drinks kept Rosie busy. She went to help Jenny every day. Walking with the rocker on her foot supporting the cast on her leg was easier now she was used to it. Eric took her to the park in the morning and either he or Linda came to take her home at the end of the day.

Jenny taught her the best way to make sure she gave the correct change to customers.

"This is what you do," she said. "Let's say a customer gives you fifty pence and asks for an ice cream cone and a rocket ice lolly. How much is that?"

Rosie checked the price list and said, "Twenty two pence."

"That's right. Now go in the cash drawer and take out the coins and count starting from twenty two until you get to fifty."

Rosie took a one penny piece, a two penny piece, a five pence and a twenty pence counting aloud twenty-three, twenty- five, thirty, fifty!"

"There you are, you see? You have the right change in your hand without having to do a subtraction in your head. Do you think that's easier? I do."

"I wouldn't ever have thought of doing it that way," Rosie said, "but, yes it's easier. It's faster. Can I do another one, please?"

They practised a few times until Jenny was sure Rosie was confident. She stood behind her, watching, when she allowed Rosie to serve her first customer. For Rosie it was like playing at shop, but for real, with real customers, and real things to sell. She did the counting out of change aloud as Jenny had taught her and the customers smiled at her and commented on how well she was doing.

Rosie wasn't allowed to touch the coffee machine that frothed up the milk but not many people wanted hot drinks. Only the early morning dog walkers and fitness runners came for coffee in the mornings and Jenny served those people. But helping with ice creams gave Jenny more time to make up the lunchtime sandwiches and set out her fancy cakes on the cake stand for later in the day.

John kept his eye on the bench whenever he was working in the vicinity of it. He brought his own packed lunch and sat at one of Jenny's tables instead of his favourite corporation green bench because, he said, if he was sitting on the bench it might put people off either taking the book or bringing it back. Rosie kept a lookout on the bench too to see when Treasure Island had been taken and when it came back and it was strange, she said, how she never managed to see anybody in the act of taking or returning it. It all happened mysteriously, as if it was part of the magic.

But it was definitely happening. The notes people left for them proved it. After Hugo Fairclough, the next person to read Treasure Island was Stephen Whitlock. His note said he hadn't read a book for years. He wrote that he'd been feeling down in the mouth after being made redundant and had come into the park just for a bit of fresh air. He saw the book on the bench and read Rosie's and Hugo's notes. Then he thought, why not give it a go? He enjoyed the read, he said, and it made him forget to be sad. Jenny explained the meaning of down in the mouth when John asked. She stretched her mouth into the shape of a downward arc to demonstrate.

The reader after that was Molly Stott. Her note brought tears to John's eyes. Molly said she had been a poor reader when she was at school. Her childhood had not been a happy one and she was bullied a lot. She thanked Rosie and John for giving her a second chance and encouraging her to try again to read the book that had beaten her when she was a schoolgirl.

Then there was Michael Drummond. Michael was a regular in Myrtle Park and was often to be seen with his photographic equipment taking close ups of birds and squirrels. He even came into the park at night sometimes to capture a striking sunset or a moonlit scene. Occasionally he had his photos in the Kingsley News and he'd write a column to accompany his latest masterpiece. The note he left behind said he'd taken the book to read because he admired new ideas and was happy to encourage the young people who had thought of it. An added bonus, he said, was how surprised he was that he'd enjoyed Treasure Island. Nobody wrote stories like that any more, he said.

Police Constable Colin Radcliffe came next. His note was full of admiration for the community spirit shown by Rosie and John and how he planned to buy a copy of Treasure Island to read to his own children if he ever became a father.

One afternoon, after the lunchtime busy period was over Rosie was outside the kiosk eating a bowl of salad Jenny had especially made for her. Jenny was thinking of branching out with something different on the menu in future, she told her, and would Rosie like to try? Rosie was enjoying the tuna, pasta and sweetcorn mixture when she noticed a familiar figure coming toward the tuck shop. The woman was carrying the book.

"Hello," the woman said. "It's Rosie Mirren, isn't it?"

"Yes, Miss Hewitt," Rosie said.

"And you are the young lady who leaves the book on the bench."

"Yes, Miss."

"Do you mind if I sit with you for a moment? Don't let me stop you enjoying your meal. It looks good. What is it?" Eleanor Hewitt said and put Treasure Island on the table.

Rosie explained Jenny's plan to bring in some new foodie ideas. "It's very good," she added. "I like it a lot."

"And I like very much what you and your friend are doing, Rosie. What a lovely idea. And you did all this with that big pot on your leg. What happened?"

"I broke my ankle, Miss, learning to roller skate. But it doesn't hurt so much now. Anyway, while I was at home I could do some reading."

"You've always loved books, haven't you?"

"Yes, Miss."

"So have I, dear. So have I. What was it that made you choose Treasure Island?"

Jenny came out to see if Rosie was all right, then recognised Eleanor Hewitt from Kingsley Primary School.

"Hello," Jenny said. "Is there anything I can get for you?"

101

Eleanor Hewitt asked if there was any more of the salad Rosie was eating.

"You're in luck," Jenny said. "I made extra just in case but I haven't worked out how much I should charge for it yet." They agreed on a price and Jenny brought it out. "Are you still at the Primary School?" she asked.

"I retired last year," Eleanor said.

"I bet you miss it."

"I do. I miss the children. Rosie here was one of my pupils, weren't you Rosie?"

"Yes, Miss."

"So, it's been a lovely surprise to find Rosie's book waiting on the bench for people to take it home to read."

"It isn't my book, Miss," Rosie said. "It's John's."

Jenny explained how the two of them had come to be friends before they devised the book on the bench plan.

"Then that partly answers my question. You chose Treasure Island, Rosie, because . . . well, because, why?"

"Because I get my books from the library, Miss Hewitt. I couldn't use one of them. John had a book that we could use."

"And did you read it?"

"Did they read it? The pair of them never stopped talking about it. I've heard enough *Yo-ho-hos* to last me a lifetime," Jenny said and winked at Rosie.

"It was your choice of book that made me pick it up, Rosie," Eleanor said.

"Really? Why?"

Eleanor Hewitt picked up the copy of Treasure Island and handled it as if it was a priceless piece of china.

"I've loved reading since I was a child," she said. "When I won an essay writing competition at school I was thrilled when the prize was a book token. My mother took me to the book shop in town to choose. I loved the smell of that shop. I still do."

"Here in Kingsley?" Rosie asked.

"Yes, it's still there. All the children's books are down the stairs in the basement. My mother waited upstairs and I went down to make my choice. I chose Treasure Island. I don't remember the exact price back then, but it would have been even less than one shilling."

"Less than five pence?"

"Yes. The illustration on the front of the dust jacket was very much like this," she said and stroked the front of John's book. "I noticed it straight away when I saw it lying there on the bench. In the shop I took the book I'd chosen for my prize up to the ground floor and handed it to the shop assistant. *This is the one I would like to have*, I said. The shop assistant gave me a strange look. *Are you sure?* he said. *This is a boys' book*."

"Was it? I mean, is it?" Rosie said.

"My dear Rosie," Eleanor said, "when that young man said that to me I was more determined than ever to read it."

"So would I, if somebody said that to me," Rosie said.

"I have written a small note as you wished to go with it and I would like to thank you so much for bringing back to me such precious memories."

Eleanor Hewitt looked as if she was in a daydream, Rosie thought, as she noticed the smile on her former teacher's lips and the faraway look in her eyes.

"I'm glad," Rosie said. "It makes me happy when the magic works."

"It certainly has worked, Rosie. I've always believed there's no such thing as books meant only for boys or girls."

Rosie Mirren and Eleanor Hewitt finished their bowls of pasta salad together. Jenny made tea and brought it out. Rosie had a lemonade.

"I think these new salad bowls might be a hit," Jenny said. "But it will mean more washing up for somebody. I wonder who?"

"I'll be back at school by then," Rosie said and laughed.

"I took the opportunity to read all the other notes inside the book," Eleanor said. "Isn't it simply wonderful that people have done exactly what you asked for? They've shared quite a lot of personal information about themselves. I admit I'm surprised by that but absolutely delighted. I would love to meet them."

"Why don't you?" Jenny said.

"I'm not sure how that might be arranged. How would we contact them? We don't know where they live. I suppose we could try the telephone directory as we have their last names on the notes they wrote but that would be rather hit and miss, wouldn't it?"

"Well, if I were you," Jenny suggested, "what I'd do is put up a notice somewhere here in the park. They obviously all come in here so, say you put it either on the bench or here at the tuck shop. Just a date, place and time should do it."

"That's perfect," Eleanor said. "What do you think, Rosie?"

Rosie was way ahead of them.

"Here at the shop is the best place," she said. "Then, if they're a bit embarrassed about meeting new people they can just buy an ice cream and walk away. We won't know who they are, will we? We don't know what they look like. Except for Mr Fairclough. Make the meeting for the day of the Kingsley Show when there's always loads of people about and lots of things going on."

Chapter Fifteen

The Kingsley Show was an annual event that had been taking place for almost a hundred years, having begun in eighteen seventy six when Kingsley was a market town, the hub of a large region of animal husbandry. An agricultural show at the outset it had grown and developed to include more than the exhibiting of cattle, sheep and other farm animals.

By the mid nineteen seventies enormous marquees housed art and craft exhibits, cake and jam competitions and flower arranging, needlework and photography, best vegetable contests and locally produced foodstuffs. Outside they held dog shows for pedigree breeds and family pets. In the lower field a large area was set aside for show jumping which always attracted huge crowds who sat along the grassy bank looking out over the field and the river beyond which formed the western boundary of parkland.

At the kiosk Jenny anticipated little change in daily sales. There'd be too much competition from the various catering vans throughout the park. Before long, frying onions and burgers would scent the air and sweet and sticky candy floss or syrup pancakes for afters. Many visitors who planned to stay for the whole day at the show brought picnics but Jenny knew that, for the older generation at least, the chance to sit away from the noisy crowds with a nice cup of tea would be welcome.

John had been darting about since he first arrived early in the morning. Chief had given him extra responsibilities and he was especially keen to do everything properly. All the marquees had been set up overnight in previously agreed locations. This always went smoothly as there was little change from year to year.

First to arrive, not long after first light on the day of the show were the larger vehicles bringing in prize exhibits of cattle and rare breeds of sheep and pigs. The animals were housed in pens in several smaller marquees erected in a semi- circle around the perimeter of the show ring to wait their turns in front of the judges. John was to make sure all the pens were floored with plenty of straw. He put much effort into spreading the straw evenly, to provide comfortable bedding for the animals. He understood how tired they must feel, he said, having to get up so early. The horse boxes came in next. They used the lower park entrance to get into the bottom field and there were other park keepers and volunteers down there organising them into their places.

All the smaller vehicles, company transits, catering and ice cream vans and private cars came in last and had to be unloaded and cleared to their designated parking spaces well before the publicised opening time. Chief worked together with the main event organisation team to check everything was going as it should.

John's next job was to put out the name cards for all the exhibitors in the flower arranging tent. Chief had given him a diagram to work from and he followed it to the letter. He liked to visit the flower arranging tent again later when the competitors had finished building their displays. It fascinated him to see the beautiful shapes they could create with blossoms and leafy sprigs and the colour combinations they put together.

The show fields opened to the public at nine-thirty. Eric and Rosie were already at the tuck shop. Linda was working an early shift and would be along later in the afternoon. Jenny was proudly fussing over her tables.

"They look very nice today," Eric said. "They always do, Jenny. But today they're extra special."

"Harry gave us permission to nip a bit off some of the flowering shrubs around the park," she said. "I mean, aren't they all fabulous this year? We've got santolina with the mauve hibiscus and some white roses John cut for me. Well, you have to have white roses in Yorkshire, don't you? And then, it wouldn't be Kingsley show here in the park without some myrtle as well."

"As I said, Jenny, fabulous."

"Thank you, Eric. Rosie and me put it together, didn't we, lovey? We've been saving jam jars."

"They don't look like jam jars now they've got flowers in them," Rosie said.

Jenny said, "Are you going to have a walk around the grounds before the main crowds come in, Eric?"

"We are, for sure. We'd like to be back here in time for the meeting, though."

A notice in bold felt tip pen inviting readers of Treasure Island to come to the tuck shop for coffee at eleven o' clock was still sellotaped to the kiosk wall by the serving hatch.

"I hope somebody comes," Rosie said. "I think Miss Hewitt will be disappointed if they don't."

"We'll have to wait and see," Eric said.

Eric took Rosie all the way around the show fields. Rosie didn't know what to look at first. There was colour and noise and people everywhere. A loudspeaker was calling out where to go to see which events and she could hear dogs barking and children shouting. There were queues for drinks and queues to get into the marquees. They had to dodge in and out of the crowds as they moved on.

The rocker block under her foot hardly bothered her at all. Her leg must have got thinner because the cast felt loose. The plaster had become softer, too and had stopped rubbing her skin sore. She could easily keep up with Eric's stride.

Gathered around one of the smaller exhibition rings they saw a crowd of people jostling for spaces to look at was going on inside the show ring. The crowd was made up of every age group, toddlers and older children, teenagers, mums and dads and grandparents. All of them were laughing. They went to see. Rosie was delighted by what they found: a demonstration of sheepdogs herding ducks across the grass, through a gateway and into a small pen. Some ducks misbehaved and didn't want to go where the dogs wanted them.

Others flew up into the air and tried to escape. Eventually there was a winner and the dog and its owner were awarded a rosette.

When that was finished Rosie had a turn at the splat-a-rat game and won a prize; she ate a toffee apple; they walked through the craft marquees and saw needlework and paintings, cakes and jars of jam, things made of wood and things made of metal. In the produce marquee there were onions the size of footballs and cauliflowers big as a space hopper. The flower arranging tent was quieter and filled with the intoxicating perfume of blossoms in so many colours and shapes and sizes it was hard to choose a favourite. She was just thinking how much John would enjoy the flowers when they bumped into him. He was watching a photographer take pictures. She tapped his arm to say hello.

"Hello, Rosie. Hello, Eric," John said. "This is Mr Michael Drummond. He's taking photos for the Kingsley News. He's coming to our meeting at eleven."

Michael Drummond laughed. "It's a meeting now, is it? I thought it was a cup of coffee we were having."

"Morning, Michael," Eric said. "Not your usual subject matter, flowers?"

"You're right, Eric. I thought I might as well while I'm here. So this young lady is Rosie. How d'ya do, Rosie?"

Rosie looked up at a tanned face towering over her. It reminded her of when she had to tilt her head all the way back to look up at her father. She'd grown taller herself since the last time she looked up at her father so this man must have been even taller.

"I'm very well thank you," she answered him politely and shook hands with him. The touch of him gave her a strange feeling, like a shiver or an ache.

"I'm looking forward to meeting all the other Treasure Island readers," he said. "What a brilliant idea you had."

"I hope they all come," Rosie said, and added,"Eric, you already know Mr Drummond, don't you? Do you know everybody in Kingsley?"

"Nearly," Eric said and winked at Michael.

Eleanor Hewitt and Hugo Fairclough were already seated outside the kiosk when they returned with Michael. Eleanor stood to meet them.

"Hello," she said. "I'm Eleanor. I'm so pleased to meet you all."

They rearranged the chairs and pushed two tables together. Jenny took their orders and she hardly had time to come back with their drinks before the others began to arrive. Molly Stott came first. She approached the group tentatively and asked if she'd come to the right place.

"Yes, love," Jenny said. "Here we are, the Treasure Islanders. Although, to be honest, I haven't read it myself yet. Since Rosie here started it off it's always gone out when I go for it. Can I bring you a drink?"

Stephen Whitlock came with his dog, an ageing chocolate Labrador called Yogi who quickly found a shady spot beneath the awning and lay down. Stephen introduced himself and made a joke about how the dog could be his cover if he bottled out at the last minute.

He'd be able to walk past the kiosk with his dog and nobody would be the wiser.

"I felt nervous too," Molly admitted. "I've never joined any kind of group before."

"You're very welcome, Molly," Eleanor said. "I'm so pleased to meet you. Did you enjoy Treasure Island? It used to be one of my favourites."

"I enjoyed the story once I got into it," she said. "I had to look up some words I didn't know but once I got going I thought it was exciting."

"Same here," Stephen agreed, "but if pirates all spoke in a Yorkshire dialect instead of a West Country one they'd have been easier to understand."

"But it was more than just an exciting story for me," Molly said. "I enjoyed the actual reading, if you see what I mean. Just sitting down with a book and feeling good about it. I didn't get very far in school."

"Well, if it's any consolation to you, Molly," Jenny said, "neither did I. Mind you, we had a tartar of a teacher back in those days. She'd wallop you as soon as look at you."

"I was never much of a book lover when I was younger," Molly said. "Now I feel I can go on and find more books to enjoy."

"If you'd like some suggestions, I'm willing to help," Eleanor said.

"Would you help me too?" John asked.

Rosie was so delighted with the way the meeting had turned into a friendly chat she was tempted to wiggle her nose at the magic developing right before her eyes. She was content just to sit and listen.

Police Constable Colin Radcliffe popped by to say hello. He was in his full uniform and looked very smart.

"I'm on duty today so I can't stay with you," he said, "but I just wanted to let you know that I wish you all the best with your idea." Gently, he tapped Rosie's shoulder. "And you, young lady, are going to be a force to be reckoned with one day."

"It wasn't just me," Rosie said. "I needed help. John gave the book and Eric helped us to read it."

"Well done to all of you. Have a good day," he said and, with a wave to them all, walked off into the show ground.

Rosie continued watching and listening to the conversations growing and developing further. She heard them telling each other about their working lives and their families and which part of Kingsley they lived. They were all still chatting when her mother arrived after her early shift at the supermarket. Linda recognised Eleanor Hewitt immediately from their meetings at parents' evenings and quickly fell into conversation with the rest.

In the way that growing children sometimes do, Rosie was aware that there were emotions swimming around inside her: feelings she didn't yet have the language to describe; feelings about people and herself. She didn't fully understand all of it. Silently, she tried to explain it to herself but couldn't find the right words. All she could come up with was words like warm and smiling and happiness.

She scrutinised the faces of all the people sitting around Jenny's tables and every single one of them was smiling, even her mother. Their appearance was lively; their eyes brightly shining; their voices sounded like birdsong on summer days in the park which, of course, that's exactly where they were. The silliness of her last thought made her grin.

When she focused on the face of Michael Drummond though, a different emotion swooped in from nowhere and replaced the happiness feeling. Something like a hole opened up inside her and sucked away all the pleasant words she'd been thinking. The new thought made her remember how, in the flower marquee, she'd had to crane her neck to look him in the eyes. The feelings that had come to her then fluttered around her body again leaving her wondering what they were. Her stomach twisted as the hole inside grew wider. What was left was a sorrowful feeling and a pain like toothache.

"What do you think, Rosie?" Miss Hewitt was asking her a question but she didn't know how to answer it.

"I'm sorry, Miss Hewitt," she said. "I haven't been listening. What do I think about what?"

"We would all like to meet again. As friends. Maybe in time we might choose another book to read and discuss afterwards. But we don't want to leave you out. It was your idea to begin with. We don't want you to feel we're planning to steal your idea."

"I don't think that would be stealing," Rosie said. "It just means the Treasure Island reading people know each other now. I don't mind if you pick another book.

We'll still keep leaving Treasure Island for more people to find."

Throughout the whole summer the number of Treasure Island readers continued to grow, Andy Bishop, John's social worker among them. He left his note as all the other readers had done signing himself as John's friend and how he was looking forward to talking with John about the book at their next meeting. John put an extra circle around the date on his calendar to remind him.

Another member of Chief's gardening team was another reader. Eddie Robinson had heard about the book on the bench and wondered what all the fuss was about. He loved the story, he said. He'd always liked pirate stories and thought somebody should make a remake of the old film.

Richard Cox, the cold drinks delivery driver to the tuck shop was the next to read Treasure Island and leave his note. He was a reader of modern crime stories, he said, and fancied a change. When Jenny told him about Rosie and John and their plan to bring magic into people's lives he'd decided to try it out. He knew it was a book intended for children but he'd never read it when he was a boy so took the chance. The language had surprised him, he said. He couldn't imagine children of today being able to cope with it on their own.

Imogen Clarke wrote that she was sorry she'd missed the meeting on the day of Kingsley Show. She'd been to Myrtle Park to watch the show jumping and on the way out had seen the notice by the kiosk window.

She hoped there might be another meeting soon and said she'd look out for news of it.

Each reader left their written messages inside the front cover of the book. There were too many of them to keep attached inside so Jenny provided a plastic storage box to keep them in. Now there were two items to leave on the corporation green bench or at the tuck shop. Jenny, John, Rosie and Eric took care of everything to see that Treasure Island was left out in the best place depending on the weather.

When Jackie Nelson joined the list of readers the magic really began to spread.

Chapter Sixteen

Jackie Nelson had recently begun working for the Kingsley News. A young journalist whose specialism was human interest stories, she arrived in Myrtle Park the day Rosie went with her mother to the hospital to have her plaster cast removed. John was working by the paddling pool in the bottom field; Chief was busy sweeping out the tennis courts; not one of the other park staff could tell her more than she already knew. She went to the tuck shop and at the window ordered a sandwich and a drink.

"I'll bring it out to you when it's ready," Jenny said.

Jackie sat at one of Jenny's tables under the awning to wait. She took out her notepad and wrote a few sentences about her surroundings. On the crown green a bowling match was about to begin and she smiled at the comfortable Englishness of the scene with players in their whites, the pristine grass surface, the murmur of voices and the dull clunk of their woods as they gathered them ready for play. The flower beds were immaculate, she noted, beautifully laid out with contrasting and complementary colours, heights and shapes. A loving hand obviously took very special care with them.

She could hear the chirping of birds nearby and got up from her seat to look at the enclosures. There were budgerigars and love birds, some calling as they perched on their choice of foliage and on branches arranged around the open space, others flitting from branch to branch twittering as they flew. On the straw covered floor of the enclosure tortoises chewed on greens, oblivious of the activity above them. The way everything looked so lovingly cared for made her smile again. She went back to her seat to make more notes.

"Here we are," Jenny said as she brought Jackie's order.

"Thank you. That looks good," Jackie said, closed her notebook and put away her pen.

"We like to give good value. Satisfied customers are likely to come again. We get a lot of regulars. I haven't seen you here before," Jenny said.

"This is my first visit," Jackie said. "I'm new to Kingsley. I would have come to the park sooner had I known how gorgeous it is here."

"It is, yes. We're lucky to have it. I love working here."

"I can imagine."

"Well, I'll leave you to enjoy …"

"Before you go, I was wondering if you know anything about the book somebody is leaving on a bench."

Jackie Nelson had asked the right person. As Jenny launched into the tale, it seemed to Jackie that Jenny probably knew the ins and outs of everything that went on in Myrtle Park. Jackie explained her interest in meeting whoever had started the 'craze' and was surprised to learn the idea had come from a ten year old girl. This was an ideal story for the local newspaper's human interest page. She decided to wait around until the child came back. She ordered another coffee and took out her notebook again.

Eric was outside in his front garden area when Linda brought Rosie home on the bus after she'd had her cast removed. She dropped her daughter off at Eric's house and watched as she ran to his gate.

"Be careful," she shouted after her. "Take it steady."

"What's this?" Eric said. "Running already?"

"She's supposed to walk carefully, Eric," Linda said. "She has to get used to balancing again."

"I see. Well then, young lady. You'd better follow doctor's orders."

"I'm dashing off to work now, Eric if that's all right with you. I can't stop for a while or I'll be late. Here, look, I bought some treats at the bakery on my way here," Linda said and handed him a large paper bag.

"Come on inside now, Rosie," Eric said. "See you later, Linda."

In his kitchen Eric opened the paper bag from the bakery while Rosie watched and waited. He slid out a cardboard box and lifted its lid.

"Wow!" Rosie said. "They look amazing."

"Let me see you wash your hands first, Rosie please. Then you can have first pick."

"Shall we save a chocolate one for John?" Rosie said. "We could take it to the park for him."

"Are you sure you want to walk up there? I have to say your leg looks like it could do with some fresh air but are you really ready yet?"

"It feels fantastic without the pot," Rosie said. "It looks funny though, doesn't it? At the hospital they told me it wouldn't take long to look like the other. They said it's been in the dark for a long time so there's no wonder it's pale. I can't wait to show John. Can we go to the park now, Eric?"

"As long as you walk beside me. No running."

"Okay."

When they came to the tuck shop Jenny was chatting with a young woman who was writing in a notebook.

"Look Jenny," Rosie called out. "My leg's so light now I feel like I'm floating."

"You'll be glad to get rid of all that weight on your leg, I'll bet," Jenny said. "Come on, Rosie. Come and sit down and I'll bring you a drink. Eric, what would you like?"

"Hello," the young woman said, "are you the girl who started the book craze?"

"Yes. Did you want to read it too?" Rosie said.

"I hadn't really thought about it, but now that you mention it, yes, I think I would. Have you got it with you?"

"No. You have to . . ."

"Just a minute," Eric said. "I can see you're taking notes. Would you like to tell us something about what you're doing?"

"She's from the Kingsley News, Eric," Jenny said, hovering in the background, unwilling to miss any gossip.

"I'm Jackie Nelson. I write the human interest column in the Kingsley News. I heard about the book on the bench and wanted to find out more," Jackie told him.

"I see. Well then, I'm sure you realise it is a fantastic story for our local newspaper. But Rosie here is only ten years old. We can't have you practically interviewing her here without her mother being present."

"Ah," Jackie said. "I hadn't thought of that. I'm so sorry. This is my first position in this job. Please forgive me. I'm sorry, Rosie. I think I let myself get too excited."

"That's okay," Rosie said. "I do that sometimes."

"We'd better leave it at that for now," Jackie said and put her notebook in her shoulder bag. "But it's been very nice to meet you. I hope your mum gets in touch." She handed Eric a business card with a phone number where she could be contacted, collected her belongings and got up to leave. "Just before I go," she added, "What do I have to do to have my turn with the book?"

"You have to keep coming into the park and look for it. We don't know what day somebody will bring it back," Rosie told her. "Then when you've read it you have to write a note to say why you wanted it."

"Ah, is that what everyone else has done?"

"Yes," Eric said. "And now they're all friends."

Chapter Seventeen

On the evening when Jackie Nelson came to number seventeen Emerald Street in to conduct the interview with Rosie and her mother she arrived with a photographer: Michael Drummond. Linda invited them into her sitting room where Jackie took a seat on the sofa beside Rosie. Michael remained standing.

"Hello again, Rosie," he said. "It's good to see you again. I'm here with Jackie to take your picture. Is that okay?"

Rosie said, "I don't know." Michael Drummond was looking down at her. His tall figure, his dark hair and eyes made her uncomfortable. She looked at her mother for guidance.

Linda nodded agreement and went to make coffee for everybody.

"I took some photos already when we were at the meeting on show day," Michael said.

"I didn't see you do that," Rosie said.

"I know. You're not the only one. Nobody noticed what I was doing. They were so busy getting to know each other."

Those same peculiar emotions Rosie had felt in the flower tent bubbled up again.

"I think that's sneaky, Mr Drummond," she said. "You should let people know."

"Ah, well you see, Rosie, that's how I like to take photos. I don't mean to be sneaky."

"Why do you like it?"

"Because I get the best pictures that way. When people know I'm taking their photo they pose."

"Pose?"

"Yes. They go stiff and put on fake smiles. They just don't look natural. It's much better to have people unaware of what I'm doing so they're more relaxed."

"Like when you take photos of birds and squirrels?"

"Yes. Exactly. You get it now?"

"I think so."

Jackie opened her pad and quickly made some notes.

"We usually have a photo to go along with the piece in the newspaper," she said. "I thought it would be a good idea to bring Michael along this evening because you already know him."

"Okay," Rosie said.

Linda came in with coffee and a glass of milk for Rosie. Jackie Nelson asked Rosie if she was ready to answer a few questions and the interview began. Michael moved around the room looking for the best angle, finally settling on a diagonal view from an armchair in the corner. He sat, fixed the lens on his camera and asked everybody to forget he was there.

Afterwards, Rosie said she'd enjoyed the experience of being interviewed. It hadn't been as scary as she'd imagined. In fact, it had been more like a friendly chat just like at the meeting at the tuck shop on the day of the show. She tried to forget about the effect Michael Drummond's presence had had on her.

Eric had the latest edition of the Kingsley News rolled up under his arm when he took Rosie to Myrtle Park the following weekend. Jackie Nelson's piece about Rosie, John and the book on the park bench was on one side of the centre pages. They checked the corporation green bench as they walked past, as they always did. It was empty. The book and the box of written comments were both missing. Another new person had taken them home. Rosie wondered if it might be Jackie Nelson who had them. She remembered hearing Jackie say she'd like to read it.

Rosie sat at a table while Eric went to wait at the kiosk window to order their drinks. Jenny was serving up dishes of pasta salad to a family.

"Morning, Eric," Jenny said. "I'll be with you in a minute. Is that the latest Kingsley News you've got there? Is Rosie in it?"

"She is. You need to come and have a look at it," Eric said. "You're in it as well."

"Me? Blimey, are they short of news or what?"

She brought out Eric's order and peered over his shoulder to look at the copy.

"I didn't know anybody was taking photos of us on show day," she said. "It's a good one though."

"Mr Drummond took it," Rosie said. "He likes to take pictures when people aren't looking at the camera."

"Does he? Well, it seems to work well, doesn't it?"

"Do you want me to stay to do some washing up today, Jenny?"

"That would be lovely, Rosie, but this time you have to take some spending money afterwards. I checked it with your mum the other day and she told me it was all right to give you a little something."

Rosie finished her drink and went inside to help Jenny. Eric said he was going for a walk to stretch his legs. He'd go as far as the museum, he reckoned, maybe down to the bottom field and along the path by the river. Then he'd come back for her to go home and wait for her mother.

By the sink in the tuck shop there was a big pile of washing up. Jenny's success with the pasta salad dishes had inspired her to do some forward planning. She had more ideas, she told Rosie, for winter soups and simple stews and she'd been doing some trials to see if her ideas would be practical with the limited resources in the kitchen.

"I brought my own pressure cooker from home," she said, "but it's not really big enough to make lots."

"My mum has one of those," Rosie said. "I bet she'd say you could borrow that if you ask her. She never uses it."

"She doesn't use it? Why?"

"She doesn't like the noise it makes. She says it sounds like it's going to blow up."

Jenny chuckled. "Yes, they do make a noise like that. I'm used to it now. Ask her for me will you, please? With two pressure cookers I could make enough for all my winter regulars."

Rosie finished washing up and put all the cups and dishes away. She said she'd like to go on to the museum to catch up with Eric but Jenny was against it.

"That's not a good idea, lovey," she said. "We can't be sure of exactly where he is just now. Your mum would never forgive me if I let you go wandering off by yourself. Then you wouldn't be allowed to come here ever again and then what would happen to the magic?"

Rosie pulled a face and said, "Okay. I wouldn't like that. I'll wait."

"Here," Jenny said and pushed a note and some coins into Rosie's palm. "Get yourself a little treat."

"That looks like too much," Rosie said.

"No, I don't think so. You've done so well these last few weeks. I think you're brave and kind and you deserve a small treat every now and then."

Rosie thanked her and waited for Eric to come back. He looked a bit red in the face when he appeared and sank into a seat underneath the awning.

"Not as young as I used to be," he said. "I used to be able to do that walk no trouble at all."

Rosie brought him a glass of water.

"Did you go to the museum, Eric? I've never been inside. Is it any good?"

"I didn't go in this time, but I'll take you next time if you like. There's all kinds of things in there to look at.

"What kind of things?"

"Clothes that people used to wear when we had a queen called Victoria. Fossils from the time when there were dinosaurs. Fancy china teapots and exquisite furniture, so fine it looks too posh to sit on. There are

126

some beautiful paintings too. I think you'd like the one of a lady in a pink dress."

"Thank you. Yes, I'd like to go and see that painting."

"Come on then, Rosie. Best be off. See you tomorrow, Jenny."

On their way out of Myrtle Park, Rosie saw something that brought her to an abrupt standstill. A man with a woman pushing a small child in a pushchair were strolling in through the main entrance gates. The way the man walked made her heart jump. His long, slow stride and swinging arms brought back memories of how her father walked and how it was always a struggle to keep up with him when she was little.

"Are you all right, Rosie? Is your leg hurting?" Eric said.

"What? Oh, no. I'm okay," she said.

"You stopped so suddenly I thought you must be hurt."

She could have made up a story, a little white lie to cover up what had made her pull up. She could have pretended she had some gravel in her shoe. But Eric never told her lies. He was always honest with her and even when there were things he didn't really want to talk about he did his best to answer her questions. He faked losing at snakes and ladders sometimes but that was different and it didn't count as lying. When it came to serious subjects such as the time she asked him about John she could rely on him to tell her the truth. It was one of the reasons she trusted him. She told him the truth.

"It was that man who just went into the park," she said.

"Why? What did he do?"

"He walked like my dad."

Eric took a moment before he spoke again.

"Did you think, just for a second, that it was him?"

"No. Not really. It was just the way he walked that made me remember. Mr Drummond makes me remember things as well because he's tall."

"Ah, Rosie," Eric said. "Sometimes it isn't easy when we remember things, is it? All we can do is try to learn how to live with the memories that hurt so in time they don't hurt so much."

"Okay. I'll try."

They reached Eric's house and went inside.

"Do you fancy a snack, Rosie?" Eric said. "I'm going to have some cheese and an apple."

"Yes please. Could I have just an apple?"

"Are you still feeling a bit thoughtful?"

Rosie wasn't sure how to begin. She couldn't remember ever talking with her mother about her father. His name was never mentioned. Sometimes it felt as though he'd never existed. Yet she remembered happy times with him, like the time he took them to see a pantomime or when he lifted her on to his shoulders. Even though there were no photographs of him anywhere in the house, she remembered he had dark hair and brown eyes. She'd forgotten his voice, though. Eric said the same about losing Mrs Eric's voice from his memory. He often talked about her and there were photos of her on his sideboard and on the kitchen wall.

He told her his wife's name was Bessie and whenever he spoke of her by name he always had a faraway look in his eyes and a smile on his face. His memories of the person he'd lost were good ones. She wondered why her mother didn't have any good memories of her father. If she had, wouldn't she mention them sometimes? She decided to ask Eric.

When they went to his living room and sat on the sofa she began.

"Eric, did you ever know my dad?"

"Not really, Rosie. Not like I know you and your mum. Why do you ask?"

"Because I've heard you talk about Mrs Eric, I mean Bessie, but my mum never talks about my dad."

"Ah, now then," Eric said in a kind of mumble, "I think it might be better if you had this conversation with your mum, not me. I only ever saw your father a few times when he walked past down the street. We were never on speaking terms. So, you see, I'm not able to tell you much about him. I don't even know his name."

"I do. It's Malcolm. Malcolm Mirren. His friends called him big Mal, though."

"Did they? I didn't know that."

"Yes. When I was old enough to answer the phone sometimes, they used to ask if big Mal was at home."

"I remember he was a tall man."

"Yes. When he put me on his shoulders I could see over the top of everything."

"That's a good memory to have, Rosie."

"Yes, but I haven't got many more."

Eric put his arm around her shoulders and gave her a hug. "Try not to be sad, Rosie. Tell your mum how you feel and I'm sure she'll know what to do."

Chapter Eighteen

Early autumn colours had begun to appear in the trees around Myrtle Park. The sun was lower in the sky, barely climbing above the tallest of them. Shadows were longer but the air was still and the temperature only slightly cooler than the heat of August. Rosie was too hot in her school uniform on the first day back at school.

Eric took Rosie to the park at weekends as usual when Linda had her early shift. She didn't mention her father again to Eric nor had she managed to find a good time to ask her mother for more information about him. She still didn't know why her mother never had reason to talk about him: Malcolm. Big Mal.

She tried to put herself in his shoes and work out where he might have gone. He would probably have gone to the pub where he used to meet his friends on Friday nights. She couldn't go there to ask about him. They wouldn't let her inside anyway. Children were not allowed inside where they sold beer. Anyway, if he'd moved to a different town he would go in a different pub. He didn't send cards at Christmas or on her birthday. He never sent anything, not even a bit of money to help out so there was never an envelope where sometimes you could see the town's name stamped on it where it had come from.

There weren't any grandparents to ask, either. A long time ago Mum's father had done what her own father did: disappeared. That grandmother had died when Rosie was still a baby. She'd only been taken to see her father's parents once and she didn't know where they lived. All she could remember of the visit was a train ride and then a bus and then a long walk from where they got off the bus to a house surrounded by countryside. Since Big Mal had left Emerald Street her mother had had nothing more to do with them. Every idea Rosie thought of came to the same result: a dead end.

She knew the reading group was still growing though. Now that she wasn't at the park every day she depended on Jenny and John to let her know when Treasure Island had been taken again. There was more positive news, too. Plans for future book meetings were coming closer to home.

Miss Hewitt came to their house one evening to talk to Rosie's mother. Rosie was supposed to be watching television but she could hear them in the kitchen talking about where to have their meetings once the weather changed and it got too cold to have them in the park. They were going to take turns holding their book meetings in their homes and Eric had offered to do it too.

She asked Eric about their grown up meetings in people's houses and he told her he'd already had a word with her mother.

"Your mum was a bit concerned about you," he said. "She didn't want you to feel left out."

"I won't feel left out," Rosie said. "I'm happy the magic is happening. It's what I wanted - to put magic into other people's lives."

At school, Rosie's class teacher had read all about the book on the bench in the Kingsley News and congratulated her in front of the whole class. Rosie wasn't used to being the centre of attention and didn't know how to cope with it. She kept her head down and tried to concentrate on her school work but, mixed up in the happy thoughts about the success they were having with Treasure Island, another idea was beginning to form itself.

The god of putting things right was being kind. He was helping people. As the weeks went by she thought about it more and more and finally came to a decision. It was time to make some magic for herself. She'd have to keep it secret from her mum and Eric. She wouldn't be able to tell anybody about it, even John. If she could think of a way to make it happen she should try to find her father. Wouldn't that be fantastic?

Chapter Nineteen

John was humming a tune that played a lot on the radio. Chief had left it switched on in their work hut. He had an errand to run in town and said he'd be back later. John let the radio play on. The music was pleasing, a light-hearted tune that reminded him of summer days when his work in Myrtle Park's flower beds looked its best. Even the visiting bowling teams playing matches against the Myrtle Park regulars had complimented him when he told them he'd planned and planted it all by himself.

Autumn was deepening. He'd seen the first signs of it weeks earlier in the Birch trees behind the tennis courts. He always thought it strange that they were always the last to come into full leaf in spring yet were the first to shed once the days grew shorter. It wasn't the best place to have the tennis courts so close to Birch trees: there was always a lot of sweeping to do when they started dropping their leaves.

Now, all the trees were every colour but green. Some of the Maples were red as red can be and some of the shrubs in Chief's favourite shrubbery area were the same shade of crimson. Smaller Acers had turned orange. The Ginkgo biloba by the museum was a perfect golden yellow. Not a shitty yellow at all. It was one of John's favourites, not least because it had taken him a long time to learn its name and pronounce it properly. His mother had loved autumn. He smiled to himself and hummed louder at the memory of her love of autumn colours and her use of the word magnificent.

He stepped outside to test the air. The first week in October had brought chillier winds blowing across the Pennines from the east and he might need his jacket on to take his lunch to the bench. It always felt cooler when you were sitting still. He closed the door behind him and walked toward the kiosk. Rosie wouldn't be there any more: she was back at school now. She didn't even come with her packed lunch since she started having school dinners. He stopped his humming and frowned. He missed seeing her at the kiosk helping Jenny serve customers and checking to see if Treasure Island had come back yet.

Jenny was winding in the awning when he approached.

"Too windy for it today?" he said.

"You're right, John," she said. "We can't risk it getting torn. Better to be safe than sorry."

"I think I'll have my sandwich in the hut today and listen to the songs on the radio."

"Would you like a hot drink, lovey? How about a hot chocolate? You can take it back to your work hut with you, if you like."

"I like the sound of that," he said and started humming again while he waited.

The park was quiet. Everywhere looked deserted. The bowling season had finished. There was nobody practising on the greens and all the surrounding benches were empty. There wasn't even anybody walking their dog and, although he couldn't see it from where he stood, he knew the play area would be empty too.

He looked up to see the sky a peculiarly dirty shade of grey as if somebody had mixed some sour green in it. Thick dark clouds rolled across the sky, low and threatening. He heard a distant rumble of thunder.

"Here you are, John," Jenny said and handed him his drink. "Better be quick, lovey. We'll have rain soon. It'll be an early finish for me today, I shouldn't wonder."

He thanked her and hurried back to the hut. The radio was playing another song John recognised. He took a sip of the hot chocolate Jenny had made for him and its soothing warmth made him feel better. He knew Jenny cared about him. She was always finding ways to do nice things for him. Rosie would be coming back to Myrtle Park at her half-term break when Eric looked after her while Mrs Linda was at work. He consoled himself with thoughts of things to look forward to. He sat by the workbench and reached for his sandwich box in his backpack.

Thunder banged louder overhead. The door sprang open. Two figures rushed inside and threw the door closed behind them. John tried to stand but strong arms encircled his neck and pushed him down.

"Sit still, stupid. It's lesson time," a voice said.

"What? What do you mean? What lesson?"

"Think you're too famous now to learn something new, do ya? All over the Kingsley News with your stupid face and queer friends. Baz, show him the pictures."

The second man thrust an adult magazine under John's nose. John closed his eyes at the pornographic images and tried to turn his head away.

"Look at it, Moron," one of them said. "We know this is what you get up to in here. Playing with yourself every chance you get aren't ya? Can't touch your little girlfriend though, can ya? Criminal offence, that is. Touch her and you won't just be in the newspaper. You'll be in prison."

"I'll tell Andy," John said. "I'll tell him about you. Go away and leave me alone."

"Go away and leave me alone," the one called Nick mimicked in a girly voice. "Who the fuck is Andy, anyway?"

"He's my friend. He already knows about you two. You'll be in trouble."

"We've got plenty of magazines for him to look at too," Baz said and began spreading the explicit pictures out across John's workbench. "Maybe you'd like to play with each other, eh?"

"Stop it," John shouted.

Nick kept the pressure on John's neck and shoulders. "Andy and Rosie, eh? Fancy a threesome do ya?" he said.

A hot surge of anger rose through John's body. At the mention of Rosie's name a powerful rush of indignation coursed upward through him. How dare they say such things? He pushed against the arms holding him down. The force came from his feet, through the muscles in his legs and into his back. He lurched up, out of his seat and knocked Nick off balance, making him stumble backwards.

John straightened up and turned to face his tormentors. "Get out!" he shouted.

Baz moved forward, ducked underneath John's outstretched arm and swiftly pulled down John's work trousers and underpants, exposing him.

"Fuck me," Nick shouted. "Have you seen the size of these?"

John pulled up his clothes and roared. Baz was laughing. John drew back his arm and swiftly let fly his clenched fist. Baz staggered backwards and fell. John could see blood oozing from Baz's cheek and the side of his head where he'd banged it on the work bench as he fell. John didn't know what to do next. He didn't want to be in trouble for hurting someone. He rushed for the door and ran out.

"Get him," Baz shouted as he clambered to his feet.

Rain was falling in big, heavy drops that splattered on the path. The sky was so dark it looked as if night had come early. John didn't know what to do next but he could hear them running after him. He made for the tuck shop where Jenny would be able to help him but the shutter at the window was down and the door was locked. He ran to the bird enclosures and stopped to look behind him. They were coming. He ran on, circled the bowling green and the tennis courts and took the path leading to the bottom field. Slipping on wet stones he almost fell. He looked behind him. Still they followed. Rain was falling so heavily it felt solid and hard against his head and face. Water dripped from his hair and clothes and again he skidded on the path. He brushed past Chief's shrubbery area and racing into the lower field, passed the paddling pool and the bandstand. Keeping up pace he ran further, all along the length of the field till he came to the river bank. He stopped.

There was nowhere else to run to. He thought about jumping into the water but he didn't know how deep it was and he'd never learned to swim. Through the rain he could see them running across the field toward him. He made up his mind to apologise. He shouldn't have lashed out. He knew he was stronger than either of them, maybe even both of them together but he'd learned how to be gentle with animals and people weaker than himself. Seeing someone bleed because he had hit them filled him with fear and dread of what damage his strength could cause. He didn't want to do it again. He waited.

They attacked him from both sides. He held his arms over his head and face while they pummelled his body and his legs. They kicked him between his legs and he fell to his knees with the pain. When he moved his hands to hold himself there, they kicked his head. When he fell face down they kept up their onslaught, punching and kicking him. He brought up his knees and tried rolling into a ball but they jumped on him and kicked him again. He rolled over and managed to crawl beneath a rhododendron shrub and the wet soil helped him slide underneath. It was cold and wet but they couldn't reach him.

He knew his face was bloodied. It felt sticky. His head throbbed with pain and he couldn't feel his feet. It was hard to breathe. Even taking a shallow breath brought a stabbing pain in his chest. He closed his eyes. They were still there. He could hear them.

"We should make sure he doesn't talk, Baz."

"Do you fancy getting down on your hands and knees in the mud to go in after him? No? Neither do I."

"Can you hear me, Spazza?" Nick shouted. John groaned but couldn't speak. "Listen to me, Moron. You tell anybody about this and we'll do it again, only next time we'll do it to your little girlfriend."

John wanted to shout at them but didn't have enough breath. He lay still, hoping they'd go away.

"Do you think he heard you, Nick?" Baz said. "He's gone quiet."

"So what? He knows what'll happen if he blabs his mouth off. Let him stay where he is. He can stay there all night for all I care."

"He might not make it till morning."

"Even better. Come on, let's go. I've had enough."

John could hear them move away. They were laughing. The pain in his head throbbed like bad toothache and he wished he was at home. Cold rain water was dripping into his ear from the rhododendron leaves surrounding him and he couldn't move his arm to brush them away. His body was cold and heavy. He thought about his comfortable, warm bed and his best feather pillow. He closed his eyes again and felt sleep washing over him.

Chapter Twenty

Linda had had an early shift and finished at lunchtime. She wished she'd remembered to bring an umbrella when she saw the state of the weather waiting for her as she stepped outside. She tied a scarf around her head as she walked to Rosie's school. She was hoping to have a quick word with Rosie's teacher. The upcoming parents' evening clashed with one of her late shifts and she hadn't been able to exchange dates with anyone. She went to the school office first to explain. They rang the staff room. After a moment, Mrs Cunningham, Rosie's teacher arrived.

"Hello, Mrs Mirren," she said. "Is Rosie unwell today?"

"No. Why, has she been sick at school or something?" Linda said.

"Erm, no. I thought you'd come to explain why Rosie is absent today?"

"Absent? What?"

"She didn't come to school this morning."

"Yes she did. I drop her off with my neighbour, Eric to bring her in when I have an early start."

"Maybe that's where she is, then. With him. Perhaps she felt unwell after you left."

Linda mumbled her thanks and hurried away. Rosie hadn't said anything about feeling under the weather that morning. In fact, she'd been livelier than usual. She searched her thoughts for any sign of Rosie being different in any way. She'd eaten all her breakfast. Linda remembered Rosie checking her school bag to make sure she had her pencil case. She'd appeared perfectly happy. Fluttering nervousness made Linda pick up her pace. As her anxiety mounted she rushed across town and into Emerald Street. She ran to Eric's house and hammered on his door.

Eric came.

"Is she here, Eric?" Linda said, her questioning voice already faltering.

"Rosie? No. I took her to school as usual. Linda, has something happened?"

Linda's knees buckled. "Oh, no," she gasped. "Oh, no, no."

Eric helped her into his kitchen. "Tell me what's happened," he said.

"I've just been up at the school to see her teacher about something," Linda said in a breathless rush. "She isn't there, Eric. She isn't there."

"Just a minute, Linda. I went with her this morning the same as always."

"Did you see her actually go in?"

Eric took a second to consider. "I saw her go to the entrance. I can't recall if I saw her go inside. There's always a lot of youngsters milling about in the playground. Hang on, I remember now. She stood in the doorway and waved."

"And then she went in?"

Eric sank on to a chair. "Oh, Linda," he said. "I don't know."

Rosie was missing. A telephone call to the school confirmed that, after Mrs Cunningham asked other pupils in her class, not one had seen her in the cloakroom nor could remember whether they'd seen her in the playground before the morning bell. She was definitely absent at registration. Rosie had been missing since before nine o' clock that morning. Eric telephoned the police and went along the street with Linda to number seventeen to wait for them.

Two police officers came within minutes. One was P.C.Radcliffe who had been one of the early readers of Treasure Island. The other was a female police officer whose job it was to try keep the missing child's mother calm enough to answer questions. After establishing Eric's trusted rôle in Rosie's life and how he'd taken her to school as usual, the questions began.

"Does Rosie have any special friends at school?" W.P.C. Sarah Wilson asked. "Somebody whose house she visits?"

"No," Linda said. "There's nobody like that. Rosie likes to stay at home."

"No particular group of friends?"

"No. Not really. She likes to do her own thing."

"So, she doesn't mix well?"

"What? What do you mean she doesn't mix well?"

"I mean simply that it's unusual for a girl her age not to have a best friend."

"Are you trying to tell me there's something wrong with her? There's nothing wrong with her. She's just a quiet girl. What's wrong with that?"

Concern for Linda induced Eric to speak. "Linda, my dear," he said. "These questions might prompt you into remembering someone or somewhere Rosie might have gone."

"But, Eric, you know as well as I do Rosie doesn't go anywhere except the park."

"Myrtle Park where she leaves the book on the bench?" P.C. Radcliffe said.

"Yes, yes. She likes being with Jenny at the tuck shop. And John."

"John? Didn't I see him on show day? Wasn't he at the meeting by the shop?"

Eric said, "Yes. He works in the gardens. He's been helping with the book idea."

"We'll go there now. W.P.C. Wilson will stay here with you, Linda. Eric, will you tag along?"

They went first to the tuck shop kiosk where Jenny had just served Harry the Chief with a bacon sandwich. Jenny had pulled out the awning again since the wind had dropped after the storm and Harry was sitting outside even though it was still drizzling.

"Eric! Have you brought some company with you? Two for bacon sandwiches, is it?" Jenny said. "Now then, aren't you the policeman who wrote that lovely note for Rosie?"

"It's Rosie we've come about," Radcliffe said. "Have you seen her today?"

"No. She's stopped coming with her sandwiches at lunchtime since she started having school dinners. I miss her little face around the place. She spent a lot of time here through the summer holidays. Didn't she Eric?"

Eric nodded and said solemnly, "We don't know where she is, Jenny."

"You've been here all morning, have you?" Radcliffe asked Harry. "You would have seen her if she'd come here."

"No. I've been in town. Had a meeting with the bank manager. I've only just come back."

"And you?" he asked Jenny.

"Yes. I've been here all morning. Oh, well except for when I went to the loo. I'm waiting for a plumber to come and have a look at the toilet in the shop. It isn't flushing properly. I had to use the public toilets by the rear entrance. I keep asking when they're going to fix it for me, but . . .You mean to say nobody knows where she is? Didn't she go to school?"

Radcliffe said, "No. It looks like she skipped off."

"That's not like Rosie to do something like that," Jenny said. "She likes school. It was only the dinners she didn't care for."

"What changed? Why did she stop coming to the park at lunchtime?"

"I don't know. You'll have to ask her mother. Oh, poor Linda. She must be going out of her mind with worry. Is there anything I can do to help?"

"I understand there was another person involved with the book idea. John."

"John? Yes, he's here somewhere. Mind you, in this weather he'll likely be in his work hut."

"Where is that?"

Chief explained where to go and offered to accompany them.

"Thank you, but no," Radcliffe said. "Stay here please. Eric, let's have a look."

The door of the work shed was hanging open. Both men took a step inside. The radio was playing pop songs and the place was in complete disarray.

"Dear God," Eric said in a whisper.

"Eric, will you step back outside, please," Radcliffe said. "Wait for me at the shop. Don't say anything about what you've seen here."

He reached for his police force radio and made a call.

Chapter Twenty One

Inside John's work shed were all the signs of a serious scuffle: upturned chairs on the floor, an uneaten sandwich and a backpack next to them. A mug of spilled drink lay on its side. There were what looked like blood stains on the workbench and what appeared to be more stains on the wooden floor. Even more shocking, pornographic magazines of a sickening variety were strewn everywhere.

P.C. Radcliffe waited at the door for his superiors to arrive. Eric waited at the kiosk for Radcliffe to tell him what he should do next. He could hardly believe what he'd seen. What on earth was he going to tell Linda when he went back? He accepted an offer of a hot drink from Jenny and she sat with him under the awning out of the annoying drizzle.

"I'm sure they'll find her soon," Jenny said.

"I hope so."

"Linda isn't by herself, is she?"

"No. There's a policewoman with her."

Jenny clapped her hand over her mouth. "Dear Lord," she whispered. "What must she be going through? Let's hope there's a simple explanation when it all comes out."

Eric simply nodded. He dreaded to think what the explanation might turn out be. John, the John he knew to be childlike in his approach to everything had magazines like that in his workplace? What kind of twisted mind wanted to look at pictures like that? He stopped himself from thinking further.

They heard the sirens before they saw the team of officers come to inspect John's work place. The officer in charge of the initial investigation went with Radcliffe to join the others at the park tuck shop while examination of the hut took place. He introduced himself and outlined the order of procedures that would take place. The work hut was to be cordoned off, he said, to allow the team to do their work.

"But, I thought you'd come about Rosie," Jenny said.

"I can't give you any details," the officer said, "but we need to locate the young man who works there."

"You mean John? Isn't he there?"

"When did you last see him?"

"This morning. I made him a hot chocolate and he took it to his shed."

"And you haven't seen him since?"

"No. What's going on, Inspector?"

He didn't respond. Instead he asked Harry the same question.

John was missing. Rosie was missing. History of similar cases in the past usually led to an unsavoury outcome. Past experience was telling. The things they'd found in the shed painted a disquieting picture. It looked like there must be a connection between John and Rosie missing at the same time. Radcliffe kept his thoughts to himself.

The search of John's bungalow provided no clues as to his whereabouts. His rooms were meticulously clean, his possessions neatly stored, his clothes neatly folded and placed in drawers or hanging in the wardrobe. Under his bed they found a plastic storage box, but again, there was no incriminating evidence. John didn't possess a stash of pornographic magazines. Inside the storage box there were only mementoes of his childhood, some Marvel comics and a woman's tie-waist apron.

Mrs Midgeley, the warden stood outside with her hands on her hips waiting for the police officers to come out. Nobody had told her anything. They'd instructed her to use her master keys to open John's place and let them in. She argued against it but she'd had no choice.

"I'm not going anywhere," she said to the policeman standing guard outside John's front door. "I'm staying right here until somebody tells me what's going on. I'm responsible for all these properties. You better not go smashing things about. Poor John. He won't like it. Does he know you're all here? Does he know what you're looking for? Shouldn't he be here while you're going through his things? I'll go and get him if you like. He'll be at work. It isn't far."

"We have officers in the park now," the police constable told her.

"So, why won't you let him come home? Where is he, then? Has something happened to him? Is he all right?"

"I'm not allowed to tell you anything," was the only answer she got.

She waited until the officers came out and she moved forward to lock up John's door. One stood in her way and wouldn't let her. He said further investigations were needed and a specialist team was on its way. No amount of complaint and questions moved any of them to give her more information.

She went to her own home, picked up her shopping bag, put on her coat and set off to look for John at the park. She found a small group of people sitting at a table outside the kiosk. One of them was the woman who ran the little shop. One was a uniformed policeman. She approached them.

"Excuse me," she said. "I'm Sylvia Midgeley, warden at Myrtle Court. I'm looking for John. I'm worried about him. Something's going on and I don't like it. The police are searching through his home. Do you know where he is?"

"Hello, Sylvia," Eric said. He told her his name and how he knew John.

"Ah, yes," she said. "I've heard him mention you. He told me about the little girl, Rosie and you leaving a book on a bench. I saw the story they put in the Kingsley News. So, do you know what's happening?"

Eric looked straight at Radcliffe. His eyes asked the question before he said it. "She's going to find out sooner or later, isn't she?"

Radcliffe nodded. "Just the basics," he said.

"Sylvia," Eric said, "it seems that John is missing. The police are hoping to find him."

"Missing? But, didn't he come to work this morning? I saw him leaving home. He always gives me a wave."

"How was he this morning?" Radcliffe asked.

"How do you mean? He was his normal self. Just John. He loves his work here in the park. He always looks happy when he's coming here. He loves his gardens."

"But he does have difficulties. Developmental and learning difficulties, I mean," Radcliffe said. "After I borrowed the book and brought it back I noticed there was something very different about him."

"So, what?" Jenny interrupted. "What does that have to do with anything?"

"I mean he might not fully realise how much younger than him Rosie is. You have to admit it's a very odd friendship," Radcliffe said.

Sylvia Midgeley saw how Jenny's demeanour changed. Her eyes narrowed, her cheeks flushed, her face looked thunderous.

"I have no idea what you're hinting at," Jenny said to the policeman, "but I tell you now that boy wouldn't hurt a fly. If you're suggesting that John has had anything to do with Rosie going missing, you'd better look elsewhere."

"She's gone missing, too?" Sylvia said. "What, both of them? At the same time? Oh, no. No, no, no. I can guess what you're thinking. There has to be a good reason. You can't possibly think that any of this is John's fault."

"The police obviously think it looks like it," Jenny said, "but I'm with you, Sylvia. There's no way John is to blame."

Chapter Twenty Two

Sylvia Midgeley left the others at Myrtle Park and although she didn't feel like walking into town at that moment, she needed some shopping. Her visit to the grocery store coincided with school coming out. There were many more parents than usual waiting outside. Huddled together in groups they filled the area either side of the school gates. She had to ask a group to step aside and let her pass without having to step off the pavement into the road.

"Haven't you heard?" one of the mothers said. "There's a girl gone missing. We've been asked to be sure to come and collect our kids today. Not to let them walk home by themselves."

"Yes, I had heard, thank you."

Sylvia carried on along the road wondering what was going to happen next. In the store she bought fresh bread, butter, some cat food, a packet of bacon and a box of eggs. Her thoughts were miles away. Instead of planning her evening meal she was thinking about John and the little girl, Rosie. She stood at the cash desk and didn't hear the assistant tell her the total.

"Are you okay?" the young woman asked.

"Excuse me?"

"Do you need some help with your packing?"

"What? Sorry, I wasn't paying attention."

She paid the cashier and, still lost in her thoughts, left the store. She couldn't leave things up in the air. She couldn't just sit back and do nothing. Somewhere, John must be needing help. Maybe the missing girl had gone to look for him.

At home, she hurriedly put her shopping away and went out again. She made her way back to Myrtle Park. The tables out front of the kiosk were all empty but Jenny was clearing away mugs and plates. When she saw Sylvia approaching she stopped.

"Hello again," Jenny said. "What can I get for you?"

"I'd like two coffees, please, one for yourself, and a few minutes of your time."

Jenny brought Sylvia's order and sat with her.

"What is it you want to say?" Jenny said.

"I want to talk to you about John, if you don't mind."

"Go on."

"I've been thinking about what everybody except you and me seems to be thinking."

"So have I. I can't stop thinking about it."

"He's such a kind young man. I can't believe he has it in him to harm anybody let alone the little girl."

"That's how I feel. I'm worried about him. Something must have happened to him. People don't just disappear into thin air."

At number seventeen Emerald Street W.P.C. Sarah Wilson had made tea and was attempting to persuade Linda to have some when there was a knock at the door.

"It isn't a good time," Sarah told the two women standing on the path. Across the street a small group of neighbours had gathered, all looking towards number seventeen and the police car parked outside.

"Who is it?" Linda shouted from the living room.

"It's me," Jenny shouted back. "Jenny and Sylvia Midgeley, the warden at the new bungalows near the park."

Linda wanted them to come in. W.P.C. Wilson wasn't sure that would be a good idea but Linda insisted.

"We don't need any tea, thank you," Jenny said when it was offered. "We just wanted to sit with Linda while she's waiting for news. I should think she'd appreciate a friendly face just now."

With her arms tightly folded across her, Linda was sitting on the edge of the sofa when the two women went into her living room. Her face was pale, her back rigid as if she was about to leap up from her seat.

"Linda," Jenny said. "You haven't met Sylvia before, have you? We just thought you might need a bit of company rather than sit here on your own." Linda nodded. "I can imagine you probably won't feel much like talking right now, so, we'll go away again when you've had enough of us."

"No, no, it's okay," Linda said. "I'd rather not be on my own. This waiting is just too. .." Her voice tailed away and she couldn't finish the sentence.

"Can I say something?" Sylvia Midgeley said. She waited for Linda's agreement. "I just want to say that I think there's going to be a really simple explanation."

She saw the fear in Linda's eyes and added, "I won't say any more."

"I'm surprised Eric isn't here with you," Jenny said.

"He was here earlier," Linda said. "Then he went up to the park with a policeman. The one who read the book."

"Yes. I saw them together," Jenny said.

"What were they doing?"

"Looking for John."

"Why?"

"John is missing too."

"What? Just today? Oh, my God. You think they might have gone somewhere together?"

"They're trying to find out."

Linda jumped up and ran upstairs to the bathroom. They could hear her being sick. When she came back down she looked paler than ever. Jenny sat beside her and held her hand.

Outside, the curious crowd had grown bigger. Rumours were rife. Anybody passing by could have heard what they were saying, what they were assuming, and who they were blaming, including the mother of the child for allowing such a peculiar friendship to develop.

As they walked along the street from Eric's house, Radcliffe advised Eric not to respond to what the crowds were speculating. He reminded him not to speak about what they'd seen in John's work hut and not to repeat anything he'd heard just then out in the street. If the crowd of rubberneckers became a problem they'd be moved away, he said. The last thing the child's mother needed to hear was people stirring up accusations. At number seventeen W.P.C. Wilson let them in.

Jenny moved away to let Eric take her place beside Linda who was quietly sobbing. She reached for a box of tissues she saw by the fireplace and handed it over. Eric pulled one out and gave it to Linda.

"Here, blow your nose," he said. " you don't want to give our Rosie a fright when she comes back, do you?"

Linda tried a smile. Trying to stay hopeful was so difficult when the waiting, the not knowing was tearing her apart. They sat in silence as the minutes ticked by. P.C.Radcliffe went into the kitchen. He stood by the window keeping a lookout for anybody approaching the back of the house. W.P.C. Wilson joined him to wait for news.

In Linda's living room nobody knew what to say so they continued sitting in silence. The minutes turned into an hour. Drizzling rain had stopped but the sky was still overcast. October daylight was beginning to fade. It would be almost dark by six thirty. A missing child in darkness was an even more terrifying prospect.

They heard a crackling radio noise coming from the kitchen. Then there were voices but they couldn't make out what was being said. Linda stiffened and gripped Eric's hand even tighter. The voices continued. Eric put an arm around Linda. She sat with her eyes closed.

Jenny tensed with anticipation and Sylvia took a deep breath. The voices stopped.

Radcliffe rushed into Linda's living room. "She's been found," he said. "She's fine. She's well."

"Oh, thank the Lord," Jenny said.

"Where?" Linda said.

"She was in Leeds."

"Leeds? How on earth did she get to Leeds?"

Sylvia Midgeley reached out and patted Linda's arm.

"Well, I'll be away then," she said. "I'm so pleased for you, Linda but you won't want a house full when your daughter comes in through the door. I'll leave you in peace."

"I'll come with you," Jenny said and got up to leave.

"Thank you for being here," Linda said. "Thank you for thinking of us."

"There'll be special treats for both of you next time I see you in the park," Jenny said. "Are you ready, Sylvia?"

"Right behind you. Do you want to come to mine? I want to make a phone call straight away. I think Andy Bishop needs to know about what's going on."

Chapter Twenty Three

W.P.C. Sarah Wilson helped herself to one of Linda's tissues and went back to the kitchen to use it out of sight of the others. Linda was sobbing loudly with relief.

"Where is Rosie now?" Linda said, her breath shuddering as she spoke.

"On her way home. Officers are bringing her in a police car." Radcliffe told her. "They'll be about half an hour."

"What was she doing in Leeds?" Jenny said.

"I think we've yet to find out," Radcliffe answered. "I suspect there's quite a lot more we need to discover."

Eric said, "Was she on her own?"

"I believe so. Again, there's more we need to know."

They spent the longest ever thirty minutes throwing questions around the room, not finding answers then asking more questions. Radcliffe's radio sounded again and the room quietened, each of them hungry for updated news.

"They're ten minutes away, Linda," Radcliffe said. "Sarah, would you go outside and move those people away before they get here?"

"What people?" Linda asked.

"It's just a group of concerned neighbours," Eric said. "Nothing to worry about."

Rosie sat in the back of a police car with a female officer beside her. The policewoman had been kind. She'd listened to her explanations and seemed to understand. There'd been a lot of phone calls going on as she'd sat in an office at the police station on the outskirts of Leeds. She could tell they were talking about her but the policewoman assured her she wasn't in any trouble.

Rosie sat quietly, looking out of the car window, watching the traffic and streets of houses and shops flashing by. The god of putting things right had let her down but worse than that, she'd ended up causing problems and making her mother worry. Everything had gone so wrong that she'd had to get the police involved.

"You're very quiet, Rosie," the policewoman sitting next to her in the back said. "Are you okay?"

Rosie sighed. "Not really," she said. "I want to go home but I wish I'd gone to school this morning like I was supposed to. None of this would have happened then. Now everybody will know what I did. Even my teacher and all the neighbours. My mum won't like that."

"Rosie, I think you were very brave in your intentions. You made a mistake the way you did it. That's all. Anybody who met you would be able to tell you're not a bad kid. You didn't mean to upset people."

"But, I bet that's happened anyway. I've hurt my mum. I bet I've hurt Eric as well. And John."

"Eric is the elderly gentleman who looks after you until your mum comes home from work. Have I got that right?"

"Yes."

"I'm sure he'll be just as happy to see you home safe and sound as your mum will be."

"I hope so."

The way to Sylvia's home took the two women past John's place. A solitary police constable stood by the door. The search team had left.

"Ah, Mrs Midgeley," he said. "I've been waiting for you. You can lock up now. We're done here."

"What do you mean, you're done?" Sylvia said.

"There's nothing more to do here. They've found the girl, haven't they?"

"Yes, but John is still missing."

"Sorry, I can't help you with that. He's probably just taking a day off. Right then, back to the office for me. Paperwork to do."

After she'd had a quick look around John's rooms and locked up, Sylvia invited Jenny into her own kitchen and made the call to Andy Bishop.

"Andy, it's Sylvia here," she said. "I'm glad I've got hold of you. I think you should know that John is missing. We've had the police here searching his rooms and at his work hut in Myrtle Park. They put cordons round it. Even Harry wasn't allowed in. Nobody knows where John is. I'm so worried about him. Can you come? You know where I am." She put the phone down and went to join Jenny in the kitchen. "He's coming here."

"Who is he?" Jenny said.

"John's social worker. He's been looking after John's case for years."

"His case? What do you mean by case?"

"It's what they call their charges. Andy is like a kind of guardian to John. Well, you know John is going to need someone looking out for him for the rest of his life."

"I hadn't really thought about that," Jenny said. "I thought he just had a bit of help from the council. I've heard him mention an Andy but John has always called him his friend. Yes, that's right. There was an Andy borrowed the book and signed himself as John's friend. I didn't realise."

"Andy takes John out every now and then. In between times he keeps in touch with me in case I've noticed anything he should know about. He called me about John meeting Rosie and her family after John mentioned them to him. I told him what I knew at the time. Shall we have that cup of tea now? And a bite to eat? I haven't had anything today since breakfast, what with one thing and another. I could manage a sandwich now."

W.P.C. Sarah Wilson was on her way out to speak to the crowd outside and move them on when her police force radio chirped. She took the communication into Linda's kitchen where she could concentrate and make notes to report back later. The message was coming in from the station in Leeds where Rosie had presented herself earlier that afternoon. Wilson was being given the major part to play in filling in the gaps in Rosie's story to help the family understand what had happened and why Rosie had travelled to Leeds. The girl might be too stressed to go through it all again, it was suggested. It would be better if, when the girl came home, there was someone present who knew the whole story. Wilson accepted the responsibility and made a separate note in her handbook: wouldn't it be even better if there were officers specially trained in this kind of thing? She would mention it to the boss when she got the chance.

She listened intently and made copious notes. She couldn't help the lump that formed in her throat and when the call was over she needed a tissue again. She walked through the house to the front door, went outside and crossed the street. Several people blasted questions at her immediately all at once like a firing squad.

"It's that weirdo in the park, isn't it? He's got her."

"They shouldn't let people like him anywhere near where kids go to play."

"Everybody knows he's odd."

"If they brought back hanging none of this kind of thing would happen. There's no deterrent these days."

"What was she thinking, eh? The mother. Letting a bonny young girl spend time with him. I mean, what kind of a parent does that? Everybody knows he's not right. They didn't put that in the Kingsley News, did they?"

W.P.C. Wilson held up her hands to quieten the din.

"Rosie is safe and well," she announced. "We need you all to go on home now."

"Have you caught him, then?" someone asked.

"I don't know where you've been getting your information from but you're wrong. You've all been jumping to conclusions and getting it completely wrong," Wilson said. "Now move along, please. There's nothing to see here. You're disturbing the family."

Reluctantly and muttering about the need to apprehend the culprit, the crowd began to disperse just as another police car turned into Emerald Street.

"That's her," somebody shouted. "She's in the back of the car."

Sylvia poured another cup of tea for Andy. She put it down on a side table beside him in her living room.

"Andy, this is Jenny. She runs the shop in the park."

"Hi," he said. "Yes, I've seen you there. Now, both of you, tell me what's been going on, please."

They brought him up to date with the events of the day and how and where Rosie had been found.

"But we're both worried about John," Jenny said. "It's not like him to go off without telling anybody. He has such regular habits, you know. That's how he copes with his life. It upsets him to have to deal with change."

"Yes, I know," Andy said.

"The police assumed he must have something to do with Rosie missing too."

Andy rubbed at his forehead, deep in thought.

"You said the police had cordoned off his work shed. Is it still off limits?"

"I don't know. But why did they need to put them there in the first place? What were they looking for?" Jenny said.

"They stopped searching his house," Sylvia offered. "That's what the copper told me. He said they were all done. I checked to see they hadn't left his things in a mess before we came away."

"I'd like to see for myself. Is that okay? And in John's shed, if we can get in."

John's bungalow was neat and tidy. Nothing was out of place. In his kitchen the sink drainer was carefully stacked with a set of breakfast dishes. Andy noticed John's wall calendar. He flipped the pages and looked at previous months.

"Look," he said. "Look how John puts circles around his special days. These ones are his meetings with me. Look at this here. He's kept a record of Treasure Island going out and coming back. All listed at the side here. And here's number 17 Emerald Street written in red pen."

"That's where Rosie lives," Sylvia said. "I asked him about that myself."

"There's nothing for today. No circle. He wasn't planning to go anywhere today. If he was, it would be marked on this calendar. I'm sure of it."

"You're right," Sylvia said. "It's part of his routine."

Andy said, "We need to get a move on."

The women followed Andy towards the park. Evening dog walkers in the street stared at them as they hurried along, Andy at full pace running, Jenny and Sylvia trying to keep up with him. The work shed was still behind police cordons, closed and padlocked.

"They've all gone home by now," Jenny said. "Even Harry. He sometimes stays back for a while before he leaves. What next?"

"I think I'll go home as well," Sylvia said. "I'll keep a lookout for John in case he comes back there first."

"I'm going to Emerald Street," Andy said. "They might know something we don't. I'll call you later."

Jenny said she needed to leave too. She was out of breath from running and said she couldn't do any more. There was a bus home due in five minutes.

"You'll be faster without me, Andy," she said. "I'll call Sylvia later for news."

Chapter Twenty Four

Rosie stepped out of the police car, ran up the steps into the house, threw her school bag to to the floor and herself into her mother's arms.

"I'm so sorry, Mum," she blurted, "I'm so, so sorry."

Linda held her daughter tight and cried with her. With arms around one another they walked into the sitting room and flopped onto the sofa. W.P.C. Wilson wiped another tear from her eye and left the room. Eric choked back on his own watery eyes and Radcliffe stood watching and smiling.

"Eric, would you put the kettle on, please? I could do with that cup of tea now," Linda said.

"How about you, Rosie?" Eric asked. "What would you like, love?"

"I'm not bothered about a drink just now, thank you, Eric. They gave me some orange juice at the police station. I'm hungry, though."

Linda said, "How about some toast, Rosie? Eric there's some bread in the bread bin. Rosie likes lemon curd. It's in the fridge."

W.P.C. Wilson stood on the front doorstep of number seventeen making sure the remainder of the crowd moved away. The small group raised a round of applause when they saw her. She smiled and gave them a little wave but the memory of how quickly their gossip had turned to accusations soured the contentment of a satisfactory outcome. Still, the little girl was safe and that was all that mattered. She went back inside.

Rosie was on the sofa eating toast, her mother beside her. Both looked much less worried. Wilson had experience of what might happen next.

"How are you feeling now, Rosie?" Wilson asked.

"I feel tired," Rosie said.

"Could I have a word, Linda?" Wilson said and led the way to the kitchen. Linda got up and followed.

"What is it?" Linda said.

"There's no cause for alarm. I just wanted to point something out. I've attended similar situations before and seen how, after the shock wears off, children can get very sleepy. Rosie has had a kind of shock, a fright if you like."

"Oh, yes, I understand that. That's exactly what happened when she broke her ankle in June."

"Did she? I didn't know about that. She's recovered very well."

"She has. I can tell by the look on your face there's much more you want to ask me," Linda said.

Wilson smiled. "You're right," she said. "I'd like to suggest that you don't ask your daughter too many questions tonight. I know how much you must need to know what she's been doing today. I can give you the details. Let her tell you what she wants to. Let her say what she's able to say just now. I can give you the rest of it."

"You're telling me to be patient," Linda said.

"Not telling, Linda. Advising. I guess you won't get much sleep tonight but Rosie needs to feel safe and comfortable in her own bed. I think it would be wise to prepare yourself not to have all the answers you're looking for straight away."

Linda sank into a chair at the kitchen table and put her head in her hands. Wilson waited. Linda cleared her throat and said, "I think she was looking for her father, wasn't she?"

"Yes."

"Eric told me she'd been asking him about her dad."

"Recently?"

"Yes. He can tell you exactly when. I think she's mentioned him a few times. Things she's seen lately have reminded her of her dad and brought back memories."

"Didn't she come to you about these things she'd seen?"

"No, she didn't. I don't know why not. She loves Eric. She thinks of him as a grandfather. She doesn't have anybody else."

"It could be that she didn't want to upset you with her questions about her father."

Linda hung her head. "She should feel she can talk to me about anything that's troubling her."

The kitchen door opened and Eric popped his head through.

"Sorry to interrupt, but …"

"Is it Rosie?" Linda said and jumped up.

"She looks completely worn out, Linda. I just thought you'd want to know."

Linda took Rosie upstairs and ran a bath for her.

"It's too early for bed," Rosie said.

"I know. It's just to help you feel a bit better. When you're ready put your dressing gown on and you can come back down if you want to."

"Okay. Will Eric still be here?"

"I don't know. Would you like him to stay for a while?"

"Yes. I want to say sorry to him too. I forgot earlier."

"I'll ask him to wait for you."

"Is she all right?" Wilson asked when Linda returned downstairs.

"She's having a bath. She asked if you'd stay for a while, Eric. She wants to say something to you."

"Did she offer you any information about where she's been?" Radcliffe asked.

"No, and I didn't ask."

"Would you like me to tell you what I know?" Wilson said. Linda nodded. Wilson took out her notepad and began. "She walked into the station and asked for help. At first they thought she'd been accosted she looked so distressed. She said she didn't have enough money to get home to Kingsley and could the police help her to get home. A female officer took her to a private room and encouraged her to say what she'd been doing. Rosie said she'd been looking for her father who, she thought, lived there. She'd first travelled by train from Kingsley and then a bus out to the estate where she thought he might be. She couldn't find him and had only enough money left for the bus back to the city centre. She also asked if we could get her back before school came out so her mother wouldn't be worried."

"Oh, Rosie," Linda said. "You poor girl."

"We can sort it out," Eric said. "Don't worry. We'll make everything all right again."

Knocking at the door interrupted them. Wilson went to see. Andy Bishop came back in with her.

"Forgive me, please, for troubling you," Andy said, "but I'm concerned for John's whereabouts. I saw there was still a police car outside here so thought this was the quickest thing to do. I'm John's social worker. I know he's being bullied by two individuals. They're particularly nasty types. I know who they are and I wondered if they might already be known to the police."

Chapter Twenty Five

John stirred. He shivered. Cold and wetness all around him numbed his senses. For a second the discomfort of being cold and wet was all he could feel. He knew he was lying on his side. Something wet was scraping his face. The memory of where he was hiding returned slowly and as he regained consciousness he tried to move his legs.

Pain surged through him. He lay still to gather strength and concentration to try and shift position. Again, pain stopped him. He attempted to open his eyes. He could see nothing. It was dark but he didn't know what time it was. With his free arm he pushed away a lower branch of the rhododendron shrub he was underneath and the following splash of cold water in his face shocked him into full awareness.

He was hurt, badly hurt. He brought his hand to his face to feel for cuts. His forehead was sticky and, when he slid his fingers across his nose, he could feel that one eye socket was puffy. The eye was completely closed. He'd been awake earlier, he remembered. It was still light then and he'd been able to hear voices. He'd stayed perfectly still, pretending to be unconscious and waited. He remembered their threat to hurt Rosie. He had to make sure that never happened but he didn't know what he should do.

First, he had to get out from under the shrub. If he could turn onto his back he might be able to use his legs to push himself out from under the bush. He tried to roll and yelped at the pain in his chest. Even taking a breath sent pain stabbing through him. He gasped for air and tried again. His body wasn't working the way he wanted and he stopped to think. He tested his leg movements. He could move his right foot on the side he was lying on. When he tried to move his other foot pain ripped at his leg.

He fought to keep focussing on a plan to get out. He pushed with his good leg and his body slid a little on the wet soil. He gritted his teeth against the pain in his chest and managed to twist further to his right. His foot found purchase against something hard and he pushed again. Gradually, little by little he manoeuvred his body out from under the rhododendron shrub and onto the grassy field. He lay on his side, panting, his head throbbing, searing pain burning through his body.

Myrtle Park was silent and still. And very dark. He listened for sounds of people but there was only the wind rustling dry leaves in the trees and the hiss of water in the river. Nobody would know where he was. Nobody would be able to come and help him. There wasn't even a chance that somebody out walking their dog might see him. People didn't come out walking in the pitch blackness of night. He had to find a way to help himself. He knew there was a bench on the pathway that ran beside the river. If he could somehow reach it maybe he could get on to it. He thought sitting on a bench would be better than lying in mud or soaking wet grass. But how was he going to manage getting there?

He brought his right knee up and pushed with his right hand to roll his body. He growled at the pain but pushed through it. He rested on his knees, ignoring the pain in his left leg and across his chest. If he took a minute to steady himself he might be able to stand. He tried. It was impossible. He needed something to lean against to keep his balance. Dragging his injured leg behind him, he took his weight on his right side and crawled across the grass to the nearest tree. Again, he needed to rest to catch his breath. Intense pain was sapping his energy and he felt light-headed. He hoped he wasn't going to be sick.

The parkland suddenly grew lighter and he looked up at the sky to see a watery moon showing its pale face between rolling black clouds. He could still hear the rush of river water and thought again about getting to the bench. With his injured left side pressed against the tree he used the strength of the muscles in his right leg to push himself upright. He was standing! On one leg. A sudden thought made him laugh. He was Long John, like in the story. He was Long John Silver in the moonlight and he laughed again. Then he thought about Israel Hands in Treasure Island dragging his injured leg behind him and how Jim Hawkins got pinned to the mast by the knife Hands threw. And here he was himself with an injured leg, as good as pinned to a tree trunk for balance. For the briefest moment he forgot what he was supposed to be doing and tried to take a step. A vicious stab of pain made him howl and he came crashing down on the grass.

He leaned against the tree trunk and tried to think what Andy would suggest. Andy had always helped him through every problem while he was growing up. He wished he was there beside him. He wished Rosie could make some magic for him. It was so hard to stay positive when he was so cold and so wet and there was so much pain.

"Who's there?" a voice came out of the darkness. A tall figure appeared. "Is that you, John?"

"Yes," he answered. "It's me. Who are you? I can't see you. The moon's in my eyes."

"It's Michael, John. Michael. Michael Drummond, the photographer. You know me, John. I read Treasure Island and came to the meeting at the tuck shop."

"Yes. I remember you, Michael. I've been hurt."

Michael Drummond dropped to his knees. "John, I'm going to switch my torch on to have a look at you. Close your eyes," he said.

"One of my eyes is already closed," John said. "I can't see out of it."

Michael shone his torch up and down the length of John's body.

"What's happened here?" he said. "Good grief. John, what's happened to you? Who on Earth's done this to you? You look like you've done fifteen rounds with Ali. I can see your eye is closed completely. And you're making jokes about it. You are some kind of tough cookie, John."

"Some people hit me," John said. "It still hurts. I can't get up. I tried a few times but I couldn't do it. It hurts too much to move."

"John, we need to get some help for you. Where's the nearest telephone, do you know?"

"There's a telephone box at the end of Ruby Street but Mrs Midgeley has a phone where I live. Myrtle Court. That's nearer. Why?"

"John, I don't want you to try to get up again. Please just stay as you are. We need some help to get you to see a doctor."

John groaned and said, "Can't I just go home?"

"When you've seen a doctor. Not before. I'm going to run for a phone now, John. Don't try to move any more. Promise me you'll sit still."

"Okay."

"Here," Michael said. "Look after my camera for me. I'll run faster without this equipment. I know you'll take good care of it. It's very precious to me."

"Have you been taking photos tonight? Is that why you're here in the park when it's dark?"

"Yes. I got some great shots of stormy skies and wet squirrels. I'll show them to you when I've developed them and you're feeling better. Enough talking now, John. Promise me you won't try to get up again. I'll be as quick as I can."

John put his hand on Michael's camera to keep it still and let his head rest against the tree behind him. He wondered how long it would be before help came.

Chapter Twenty Six

Heavy rain returned through the night. High winds roared across roof tops, whistling around chimneys, rattling bedroom window blinds. Linda got up to close the windows. Rosie was sleeping soundly and didn't stir but Linda hardly slept at all. A late phone call from Eric with news about where John had been found had tormented her with guilty feelings at the thoughts she'd had about him before Rosie was found safe and came home. Now Linda knew John had been the victim of a vicious attack and was seriously injured. She lay, sleepless, listening to the rain against the glass, grateful for the safe return of her daughter, worried about the outcome for John.

By morning the rainstorm had cleared away. She came downstairs in the early hours, made herself a drink and sat in the dark, thinking. So much had happened in the space of twenty four hours. At least Rosie had come to no serious harm. Poor John, on the other hand. According to what Eric had said, John had suffered terrible injuries.

As the new day dawned she resolved a fresh start, a new beginning. Her daughter was safe and at home. Her sense of gratitude was overwhelming. She had much to be thankful for.

Rosie came hurrying downstairs just before nine thirty. She rushed into the kitchen.

"Mum, I'm late for school," Rosie said. "I'll be in trouble."

"No you won't," Linda said. "I've already told them you won't be in today. They understand, Rosie. Don't worry about it. Nobody but Mrs Cunningham knows what happened yesterday. I'm staying here with you today as well. So, no problem. Are you ready for some breakfast?"

It was such an unexpected comfort to Linda that Rosie asked for a big breakfast. Her anxiety that Rosie would still be too upset fell away but she was careful not to press her daughter for further details until Rosie was ready. It was a hugely positive start to the day. Her child was hungry. There were no signs that Rosie was troubled.

"Did the police lady tell you I went to look for my dad?" Rosie said while Linda was cooking bacon and eggs.

"Yes, love. She did. She told me you went to Leeds. Why did you think he might be there?"

"Because that's where we went when he took us to see a pantomime."

"I'm surprised you remember that, but Leeds is a big place, Rosie," Linda said. "Where would you start looking?"

"Where people called M. Mirren live. They put addresses in telephone books. I remembered when Miss Hewitt thought about using the telephone book when she wanted to invite people to the Treasure Island meeting. So I looked for M. Mirren in it."

"Rosie, we don't have a Leeds directory."

"No, but they've got them all in the library."

"So, you went to the library first."

"Yes, I looked for M. Mirren and there were only two people with an M first name. There weren't that many Mirrens at all, really. I wrote the numbers on the back of one of my school books. Only in pencil so I can rub it off. Then I went to the telephone box to ring the numbers, but first I had to go a shop and buy something so I'd have enough coins for the machine."

"I see. Did you know how many coins you'd need?"

"No. I asked the lady in the shop when I bought the chewing gum."

"Right. Okay. But why did you want to call the numbers?"

"So I could hear what the voice sounded like and if it sounded like my dad talking. I don't really remember what he sounded like but I thought I might get reminded when I heard it again. I mean, if it was a squeaky sort of voice it couldn't be him, could it?"

Linda had to take a moment to digest what she was hearing. Her daughter's quietly simple way of organising her plan was staggering. A surge of love for Rosie brought a lump to Linda's throat but she fought off her emotions.

"No, you're right," she said. "Your dad has a deep voice. Rosie, I have to say I'm so impressed by what you're telling me. You've been so clever working all this out by yourself but you know what you did was wrong, don't you? It was dangerous to do this on your own."

"I know," Rosie said. "And I am very sorry."

"So, what happened next?"

"A lady answered the first call I made. I asked her if that was the right number for Malcolm Mirren and she said no. She didn't know any Malcolms. She sounded like an old lady so I tried the other number. Nobody answered but that's the one I picked. Then I went to the train station."

"How did you pay for a ticket?"

"I had some money. Jenny gave it to me for helping her in the kiosk. You said she could."

"Yes, that's right. I did. Then what did you do?"

"In Leeds I had to ask somebody where the address was. Then I had to catch a bus. The conductor helped me. He rang the bell to tell the driver to stop where I had to get off."

Linda was struggling to maintain control of her emotions. "And did you find the house where M. Mirren lives?

"Yes. It was on a hill where there were lots of streets. So I had to ask somebody again which way to go. I found it."

"What did you do then?"

"I waited."

"You stood out in the rain and waited?"

"It wasn't raining there. There was a shop and I got hungry so I bought some crisps and a chocolate bar and waited a bit more. A lady came out of the house and asked me what I was hanging about for. I told her I was waiting for Malcolm Mirren and I asked if he lived there. She said her husband is called Mervyn and told me I should be in school. That's when I got worried about being away so long. I had to wait for a bus to go back to the train station."

"But you didn't come back to Kingsley on the train."

"No. I didn't have enough money left. I should have bought a ticket that you can come back with as well but I didn't know about them."

"A return ticket."

"Yes. I was scared so I asked where the nearest police station was and went there."

Linda wrapped her arms around her daughter and kissed her.

"I am so happy to have you back safely, Rosie," she said. "Please promise me you won't do anything like that ever again."

Rosie promised and Linda breathed more easily as she watched Rosie tucking into her breakfast. It wasn't the right time to tell her about what had happened to John. It was too much for her after all she'd just been through.

"Rosie," she said. "If you had managed to find your dad, what would you have said to him?"

"That's easy," Rosie said between bites of toast after polishing off her bacon and egg. "I was going to ask him why he never bothered to send me a birthday card and then I was going to tell him off."

"Tell him off?"

"Yes. He should send money to help us. You shouldn't have children and then just go off and leave them."

Linda's tension broke. She began laughing and within seconds the laughter turned into happy tears.

Part Two

Chapter Twenty Seven

2024

It's hard to believe how many years have passed since all that happened. A lot has taken place since, as you'd expect over a lifetime. When I think back to the day I told my mother I wanted to find my father so I could give him a piece of my mind, I can't help but wonder at the precociousness of the child I was. Would I really have done it? I think I would. I'd probably do it still if ever he showed his face. I never tried to find him again. There were more important things in my life.

Mum didn't tell me about John's injuries until after Eric had visited him in hospital. John told Eric he didn't want me to see him in the state he was in. He said he didn't want me to be frightened by the mess of all his injuries. There wasn't much of him not needing treatment. His leg was in traction, he had to have his back propped up against a stack of pillows in his hospital bed to aid healing of his fractured ribs and his head was bandaged after he had emergency surgery on his eye. His right eye was so badly damaged his sight was affected ever after. Mum told me we should wait until John said he was ready to see visitors. We visited him in hospital when he gave the okay and we took him his favourite chocolate and some comics. He thanked us and tried to smile but he wasn't himself. We didn't stay long that first time. Mum told me he was probably very tired.

"Poor John has been badly beaten," she said after we were at home. "It will take him quite a long time to feel better. Even the healing process takes a lot out of you while your body is trying to mend itself. Maybe next time we go he'll feel a bit better."

But during the many visits we made afterwards he had nothing to say and seemed to have lost interest in everything. We tried to cheer him up with talk about new Treasure Islanders and the written messages they left in the box but he hung his head and looked so morose we changed the subject.

When he was recovered enough to go home Sylvia Midgeley told us he needed a lot of encouragement to build up his strength and learn to trust his legs again. She'd tried to persuade him to go shopping with her but he wouldn't be budged. He sat in his chair watching television, she said, and hardly ever stepped outside. He especially didn't want to see the photographs Michael Drummond had taken on the wet night in the park. He said that night was a bad memory and he wanted to forget it. It was best for him to get it out of his mind, he said.

"John," I said to him one Sunday afternoon in early December when we'd gone to see him at Myrtle Court and Mum had made him a chocolate cake. "If I could get up and walk again after I broke my ankle so can you. I want you to come to the park with me."

He pulled a face and said, "I can't go there."

"Why not?"

"Because somebody else will have messed with my flower beds and I won't like it."

"That is exactly why we have to go, John," I said. "We have to get you back to work before the flower beds get any worse than they already are."

That comment seemed to help.

"Are they bad?" he said. "Haven't they started getting them ready for next spring?"

"I don't think so. I think they're waiting for you. Nobody makes it look as good as you do, John."

We all walked there together that same afternoon. It was cold but fresh and dry, the kind of grey winter day that makes you feel good about having made the effort to go outside when you come back indoors with a glow on your face. John tutted his way around the bowling green and groaned at the flower bed by the tuck shop, itself looking abandoned and forlorn in the half-light of that time of year with the shutter down and a sad-looking empty space where Jenny's tables should be.

"I'd better go to work tomorrow," he said. "I can do just a bit at a time, until I'm good and fit again. Can't I?"

He perked up on the stroll back home and was more talkative. The walk had tired him, though. He flopped into his chair and closed his eyes for a few minutes.. Mum heated up the casserole Sylvia Midgeley had brought for him. A good, beefy aroma wafted through from the kitchen. John opened his eyes and sat up straight. When Mum asked him if he had any appetite, he said he would eat a good portion of Sylvia's casserole and a slice of Mum's chocolate cake, then he was going to have an early night. We waited to see how well he managed in his kitchen before we left.

Gradually he regained his enthusiasm for his gardens and love of plants. He began telling us his plans for a change of colour in the park flowerbeds. It made me happy to listen to him talking about his favourite subject. Mum bought him a book about indoor plants for a Christmas present and he was excited to find a new subject to learn about. He applied his new knowledge in his own indoor space straight away. He started with a spider plant and a kangaroo fern because he liked their names. Sylvia Midgeley then took him to a garden centre to buy a big pot so he could have a Kentia palm standing on the floor in his living room.

He came to us at number seventeen that Christmas and Mum cooked us a traditional turkey dinner. Eric brought port wine for them and a bag full of board games for us all to play. Connect Four was the new one to come out that year but the game we loved best was Buccaneer. What a great choice it was for us that Christmas. We played it all afternoon and ignored whatever was on television, even the Queen's speech, while we raced our galleons around the playing board to be the first to get to the treasure island in the middle. The treasure pieces looked quite realistic: diamonds, rubies, pearls, gold bars and barrels of rum. I'll always remember that Christmas afternoon playing at being pirates fighting for treasure at number seventeen Emerald Street in the jewel box.

Barry and Nick, the two who had bullied John since childhood, tried to deny any wrong-doing. Their denials served only to prove what liars they were. They hadn't considered how much evidence they'd left behind in John's work hut. Even though forensic investigations in the seventies hadn't reached the standards of today, their fingerprints were all over his workbench and the door handle. Blood samples taken from the bench and the floor matched exactly. Andy Bishop helped John attend an identification procedure. Nick and Baz were each sentenced to serve five years in prison for what they did. They came out after three. They didn't venture anywhere near Myrtle Park again. I remember Jenny saying she'd call the police straight away if ever she saw them coming in.

"They should bring back the old village stocks," she said. "I'd throw a lot more than rotten tomatoes at them and I'd be first in line to do it."

Jackie Nelson closely followed the court case and wrote a piece naming them in the Kingsley News. They were shamed and ridiculed in many a conversation around the town for weeks. When they came out of jail and returned to Kingsley, Mum heard they were booed in every public house they went in. In the bar nearest the park, the landlord actually refused to serve either of them. Eventually Nick upped sticks and moved away. Nobody cared to know where he went.

"Good riddance," Jenny said when she found out. "We can do without his sort."

The other one, Baz found contrition and, many years later, attempted to make amends. He was a skilled plasterer and offered his services for free during the building of the new charity, Myrtle House.

In only a very few places Kingsley is not much changed from the way it was when I was ten years old. Years of austerity and general hardship has meant that some shop units in the shopping mall are empty and boarded up. We lost two major retail stores in the high street as well as several independent traders. We even lost a few public houses. The nineteen sixties block of flats where John used to live with his mother had to be demolished because of its decay. The general hospital has needed intensive care of its own due to weakened concrete and crumbling ceilings but the jewel box still stands in entirety in its rows of precious stones.

Myrtle Park still has its crown bowling green but now there's a skate park where there used to be a bandstand. It isn't just kids who love to use it. Riders have organised themselves into group sessions and there's a seniors group who have their turn on Monday evenings. I think the oldest is a guy in his fifties. In the bottom field by the river they have music festivals every summer with big names from the music world. Locals call it Kingsleybury. West Yorkshire's version of Glastonbury, but it's minuscule by comparison. The annual Kingsley Show is not quite the major event it used to be. One of the tennis courts is now for basketball and the bird and guinea pig enclosures have been completely demolished. In their place there's a much larger cafeteria with indoor service as well as more of the kind of outdoor tables Jenny was the first to introduce.

She's still with us, is Jenny. She's still active. She's just as chatty as ever. Sometimes you can't get a word in sideways. She left the council estate on the hill when it became too much for her and now lives in one of the bungalows in Myrtle Court. She still bakes cakes. She has to use her A-frame walker to balance against standing in front of the oven but she won't give in. She still insists on using her pressure cooker as well. If she keeps on going the way she's done all her life she'll be getting her greeting card from the king soon.

It still feels strange saying king instead of queen and I know I'm not the only one who feels that way. The national anthem sounds wrong when you've been singing a different word your entire life. But everything changes and we have to learn to live with it. The sensation of discomfort I had about exchanging one word for another in the national anthem gave me a kind of small insight into how people like John feel about coping with change. In the way children cling to a favourite comfort blanket, as adults we might also object to changes thrust upon us and long for the known and familiar.

Chapter Twenty Eight

All through the eighties and into the nineties The Treasure Islanders group continued growing, nurtured by Miss Eleanor Hewitt who became a good friend to my mother. I think Mum saw her as an older sister, a mother figure almost. I know she confided in her. I remember thinking how fantastic it was that my mother had found a true friend at last. Naturally, I made out it was incontrovertible evidence of one more example of magic from the god of putting things right.

Eleanor Hewitt was a loyal friend to me too. She encouraged me into higher education and, in those days, it was possible to receive a full grant to cover university expenses. My mother would never have been able to help out financially.

"Rosie," Eleanor said to me one evening after a reading group meeting at number seventeen. "What plans do you have for your future career?"

At the time I hadn't got further than thinking about choosing my A Level subjects: English, of course was my main interest. I didn't have a clear idea of what to do after that.

"I haven't really got any definite plans," I told her.

"Whatever you choose, make sure it's something you love doing," she said. "Imagine how awful it must be having to work at something you don't really care for. I always loved my own work. But also, think about how things are changing, Rosie. These new microchips are the way of the future. One day, and I believe it will be quite soon, everybody will be using a computer."

"I prefer books," I said.

"Then find a career that incorporates both, my dear."

They were such words of wisdom from a woman who had come up through an old-fashioned system of teacher training and methods of primary school teaching. Her advice stayed with me through the rest of my school days and university education and I found the perfect occupation: librarian. I took my first, Bachelor degree at Sheffield where I met Paul who was to become my husband. Eleanor came to Sheffield with my mother for my graduation and I don't know which of them looked the most proud. Paul graduated on the same day and met my mother for the first time. Eleanor was fascinated by his choice of degree subject. A light came on inside her and shone out from her eyes. She always fizzed with excitement at the prospect of soaking up new information.

"Environmental sciences?" she said. "Wonderful, wonderful. What will the future be like if we don't take care of our environment? We must take better care of it. Over to you, young man. Get out there and do your stuff."

"I aim to do exactly that," he said.

We married in nineteen ninety when we were both twenty-five. It wasn't a grand affair. Neither of us wanted that. We both kept a close eye on the purse strings and were happy with a simple registry office wedding. Our honeymoon was a joint holiday and working arrangement.

Following the Environmental Protection Act of that year, Paul took a short, temporary posting to Wales researching waste disposal and water quality. That's where we went for our honeymoon. While he visited the Electric Mountain hydro-electric facility in north Wales and afterwards, near Swansea, a revolutionary method of recycling plastic, I was at the hotels happily reading The Pillars of the Earth and The Remains of the Day. We had what you might call date nights every night with classy dinners and the best wines to make up for not having spent the day together. When I went back to work I studied part time and gained my Masters degree in what they now call information management.

Eleanor and Mum went out on coach trips together. They both enjoyed telling me about the delights of discovering beauty spots in the Yorkshire Dales or the fun they'd had in seaside resorts like Bridlington and Scarborough. Apparently, sitting on the sea wall in Whitby eating your fish and chips is the best way ever to eat them. Eleanor bought a copy of Bram Stoker's Dracula in the bookshop in Whitby and took it in to the Treasure Islanders. It kicked them off into months of exploring horror, science fiction and fantasy. Their trip to the Brontë museum in Haworth to coincide with the Steam Punk weekend developed into an annual outing for the Treasure Islanders. Mum was inspired to re-read some of her favourite classics and Eleanor introduced her to other, less well-known titles. She also spent many evenings helping John improve his reading skills. She took him to join the library and showed him where to find books he'd like. Afterwards he went regularly by himself to find books about plants. He prided himself on learning some of their names in Latin and wouldn't talk in terms of trees like holly any more. It had to be Ilex. Foxgloves had to be called Digitalis.

Soon afterwards Eleanor fell ill. She refused chemotherapy. She told me she didn't see the point in it. She said if it was her time, it was her time and wasn't willing to put herself through the ravages of that kind of treatment for the sake of living a few more months. Strong-willed to the end, that was Eleanor Hewitt. She spent her final days in a hospice, high up in the Pennines above Kingsley. Mum and I have donated to the charity ever since.

Eleanor died in nineteen ninety six at the age of eighty one. Mum was with her, holding her hand and talking to her as she slipped away. Afterwards, Mum told me she'd promised Eleanor that, although they didn't leave a book on the bench any more, she was going to keep the reading group going and keep its name. They would always be the Treasure Islanders, discovering new treasures in the books they chose to read.

Eric lived in Emerald Street for the rest of his life and was a stalwart Treasurer Islander, taking his turn at choosing the monthly title and finding new authors to follow until he became too frail. When I was a girl I thought he was very old already because of his white hair. I remember I compared him to Father Christmas but he was only a few years older than Miss Hewitt. We loved him, Mum and me. We loved him dearly. Mum gave up her job to care for him at his home.

Caring for Eric so shortly after Eleanor Hewitt had passed away changed my mother. The caring rôle brought out something in her that I didn't see when I was young. She was much more open than in the days when she always seemed too tired to talk. I think the reading group helped her too but in looking after Eric she became John's favourite word: magnificent. She did everything for him. Nothing was too much trouble.

I was working in Bradford then at the library in the Art College. Paul was on one of his environmental study groups as part of the build-up to the next global meeting of the newly named G8 since Russia's inclusion. The name reverted to G7 when Russia was suspended after they annexed Crimea. I stayed at Emerald Street in Kingsley, back in my childhood bedroom while Paul was away.

Mum and I took delivery of a hospital bed to put in Eric's sitting room so he didn't have to bother trying to get upstairs. He was embarrassed by the commode that was delivered at the same time but Mum made a kind of screen out of an old clothes horse to go around it so he had a little privacy. She always went to his kitchen when he needed to use the commode and waited until he called her. She slept in Eric's second bedroom with the door open so she could hear if he called out through the night. She was there for him twenty four seven.

I was sitting with Eric one evening while Mum went home to have a bath and wash her hair. At Eric's he'd had the bath removed and replaced by a shower. Mum said she fancied a good, long hot soak. Eric had been having painful spasms through the day and needed the maximum dose of his medication. I went to his kitchen for the dose Mum had left with instructions and took it back for him. I was about to return his empty glass to the sink when he reached out and touched my hand.

"Rosie, will you do something for me?" he said.

"Of course I will."

"Will you go upstairs and fetch something down out of one of my drawers? It's in the bottom drawer in my bedroom. It's an old biscuit tin."

I brought it down and handed it to him.

"You open it," he said and handed it back.

I lifted the lid. Inside were documents, old letters, tiny black and white photographs of people at the seaside, bonfire and birthday parties: happy snaps from Eric's life. I wanted him to tell me about the people in the photos but he had something else on his mind.

"What is it I'm looking for?" I said.

"A piece of paper in a blue folder. I put a sticky label on it to remind me how important it might turn out to be. I think now is the right time to tell you about it."

"Is this it?"

"That's the one. Open it, Rosie."

I slid out a piece of heavy quality artist's paper. Immediately, I knew what it was. There was a handwritten message and a drawing of a train with a book flying out of a window. But it was much more than the hurried scribble Eric had described to us when he first told us about finding a book on a train. The artist had drawn himself looking out of the train window. He was instantly recognisable in his flat cap and glasses. And more yet. It wasn't a simple pencil drawing as I had expected. It was in ink with a fine watercolour wash. For a moment I couldn't speak. My eyes filled with tears.

"Oh, Eric," I said eventually. "This is the sketch that began it all. If my memory serves me, we'd talked about being kind to strangers. You told us about handing in a lost book. That's what gave me the idea and when we first made plans to leave a book on John's bench. This painting started everything. The Treasure Islanders. Everything."

"Yes. I want you to take care of it."

"No. Oh, no. I can't take this. It's a David Blakeney."

"We don't know that for absolute certainty."

"I think we do, Eric. It's probably worth a fortune."

He nodded and said, "That's why I want you to have it."

"But why me?"

"Because I know you'll do good things with it."

"Surely, you'd rather give it to your own family," I argued.

"You are my own family. You and your mother. I've known you since you were not much bigger than that piece of paper."

"But I have no right to take this. Your family will . . ."

"You're not taking it. I'm giving it. My so-called family haven't bothered about me for years. They never call to see how I am. It was always down to me to contact them. When I stopped being the first to pick up the phone I heard nothing more from them. You and your mum have done more for me than they ever did."

"I don't know what to say. Except thank you. Thank you, Eric."

"Look at the other paper that's with it."

"What is it?"

"Read it and see."

I did. Eric had written an account of how he came by the artwork. He'd included all the details, dates and everything. I asked him about it.

"It will help when you come to sell it," he said. "My letter is the picture's provenance. Proof that it's genuine. It's important to have that."

"Oh, yes. I understand."

"I have a condition though," he said and winked. "If you get a really spanking amount for it I'd like you to find a way to use the money for Kingsley. For the good of the people. Especially for people like John. Will you do that?"

"I'll do my best."

"I know you will. I trust you with it. There's my solicitor's details in the tin in an envelope. You'll need them. He knows what to do. It's all arranged. You must get in touch with him. If I'd started the ball rolling sooner I might have still been here to see it happen, before I got too ill, but . . ."

His eyes flickered and for a few seconds he struggled with his breathing.

"Can I get you anything?" I said.

"No thank you, Rosie." He lay back against his pillows and closed his eyes.

My mother came back to swap places with me but I stayed with her. Together, we sat beside him and watched him sleep. His breathing calmed and he looked comfortable. I got up and went to the kitchen to make us a drink, my head full of jangled thoughts and my heart thumping with mixed feelings flooding inside me in hot and then cold, billowing waves of deepest emotion. My dearest honorary grandfather, my daily Father Christmas, the lovely man who'd cared about me my whole life was coming to the end of his own. He knew he didn't have long and the very last thing he did was give away yet another precious gift.

Chapter Twenty Nine

Eric's funeral was attended by so many people I was convinced my childhood impression of him was true: he really did know everybody in Kingsley. People from all walks of life came to pay their respects. It was obvious he'd been highly thought of wherever he'd worked. I regretted not having ever asked him to tell me more about his life. I knew he'd worked for the town council for many years but retired early to care for his wife when she became ill. I had no idea how many lives he must have touched for there to be such an outpouring of love and respect.

Not one of his biological family came even though my mother contacted them using the phone numbers we found in the biscuit tin. They made feeble excuses for their absence: previous appointments; price of flights home. They asked plenty of probing questions about his estate, though. We followed the instructions Eric had left us and told them to contact his solicitor. I didn't know the outcome of their queries just then. I didn't ask. The executor of Eric's will would take care of all legal and financial matters relating to his estate, including the sale of his house and the art work.

Eric's solicitor contacted a specialist auction house to give them prior knowledge of the likelihood that the sale of the artwork was likely to cause a stir in fine art circles. They sent an expert to view the drawing for authentication. We held a meeting at the solicitor's office where I was surprised to discover he was none other than the grandson of Hugo Fairclough, the very first Treasure Islander. It had been a long time since I set eyes on the first person to take the book from the bench, a previously planned event obviously engineered by Eric, although I wasn't sure of that at the time.

The solicitor's offices were on the high street in a Victorian building built at roughly the same time as the town library when Kingsley first benefitted from the coming of the railway. It was a time when the town punched well above its weight, ready for the upcoming industrial revolution and a burgeoning textile industry. A stately building, it suited its current employment. You expected serious business went on inside its walls before you stepped over the threshold.

Eric's solicitor came to the reception area to greet us and led us to his room. It smelled of leather and old books and old-fashioned inkwells. It wasn't very tidy. There were stacks of papers and files piled on his desk. He had to clear some away from the leather sofa he invited us to sit on. I remember my mother said afterwards she was nervous about the meeting but he made us feel at ease.

"You're the Rosie who began the book on the bench thing, aren't you? Welcome. I'm delighted to meet you at last. I'm Julian Hartley. My grandfather, Hugo Fairclough read Treasure Island to me, you know," he said as we took our places.

"Yes, I do know," I said. "I remember him telling us."

He introduced the man sitting at the back of the room, Nigel Patterson who was wearing a face like a poker player. The first thing I noticed about him was his cold, grey eyes. He nodded at me and said an abrupt greeting. Julian Hartley moved to the window to adjust the blinds and let in a little more light. Patterson asked me to bring out the artwork. Still his eyes and facial expression gave nothing away.

I'd put the painting in a small art portfolio case with glassine paper to give it more protection. I took it out carefully and laid it on the side table Julian had already cleared. I laid out Eric's provenance letter as well. Patterson stood and pored over both, taking his time and referring to a small notebook he took from his briefcase. It struck me he was like a character from Dickens, a Uriah Heep figure stooping over the table, or a smartly dressed Fagin, long fingers grasping his notebook, piercing eyes inspecting the goods.

I admit, I had butterflies. What if his pronouncement was negative? What if Eric had made a mistake? We waited. Mum was nervously tapping her feet on the floor. Patterson looked more closely at the painting, then at his notes, then back again at the art, his head twisting from side to side like an automaton. I looked at Julian Hartley. He was smiling. He nodded at me as if to say, don't worry. My mouth had gone dry and I found it difficult to smile back at him. A lot depended on the result of this meeting. I'd made a solemn promise to Eric. We had serious plans for the future.

Patterson put his handbook away in his briefcase and cleared his throat. He looked at Hartley.

"As you might expect, I came well prepared," he said. "We contacted Blakeney's agent and asked for many questions be put to him before I came here today. I have the artist's recollections of his time at the northern art college and what he recalls of his early works. His memory is very clear on some aspects."

My stomach sank. I waited for the 'but'. Patterson turned to me and Mum on the sofa. The butterflies turned into eagles. I must have looked like a startled animal in headlights. Patterson was shaking his head. Not nodding. Shaking it from side to side. I felt as if I had a heavy stone in my stomach.

"There were certain details I was looking for," Patterson said. "I needed to see corroboration. I have that here and more besides. This account from your late friend seals it. I can hardly believe it but we have here a genuine David Blakeney. Congratulations."

He gave one of those aristocratic inclinations of his head as if I had suddenly become royalty and held out his hand. I shook it with a silly grin on my face. My mother stopped tapping her feet. When I looked into her eyes she was welling up.

"Well, I don't know what to say. What happens next?" I said.

Patterson handed me a printed sheet with an outline of the procedure.

"Take this with you," he said. "There's no rush. Fortunately your late friend's last will and testament is lodged here at this office so we can be certain you possess the right to sell. What plans do you have with the money?"

I thought that a strange question and I hesitated. Julian Hartley intercepted.

"The gift of the painting was given on condition that proceeds from the sale be spent for the good of the people of Kingsley. I myself, as executor, am bound to oversee such plans."

Patterson nodded and began to gather his things. "Excellent," he said.

Eric had thought of everything. Although he'd voiced regrets about not having started the ball rolling sooner, as he put it, he'd nevertheless put in place instructions about what he wanted to do with his sole possessions. He preempted the possibility that his will may be contested by his estranged family. He'd left them a specified amount of money from the sale of his home to be shared amongst them. The rest, including all proceeds from sale of the artwork to go into his estate which he knew would go to probate.

Patterson excused himself and said he had to leave.

"I have arrangements to make," he said, shaking hands with us again. "Exciting times ahead. We'll be in touch shortly regarding delivery of the artwork."

Julian Hartley asked me to stay. He waited until Patterson had left and asked Mum and me if we'd like tea or coffee. Reading between the lines I gathered he had much more to tell me. We chose coffee which arrived so quickly he must have had it already organised.

"Wasn't that a peculiar question Patterson just asked me?" I said. "What has it got to do with him how the money will be used?"

"Just curiosity, I suppose," Julian said. "He'll have a good idea how much it's likely to go for."

While Mum and I were drinking our coffee, Julian Hartley told us he was on the point of registering The Myrtle House charity. He handed me a file packed full of photo-copied documents.

"The file is yours to take and read at your leisure. Today, time is of the essence so I'm sorry to hurry you through this," he said. "You know already what Eric wanted us to do should we secure the funds for it. I have here the prepared governing document for a charitable incorporated organisation, a C.I.O. to be named Myrtle House, Kingsley. As the only members of the C.I.O. will be the trustees, the governing document is based on the structure for a foundation constitution, which will be registered with the Charity Commission rather than Companies House." He saw my puzzled expression and added, "You'll find everything to answer your questions in the file, Rosie. Initially, trustees will be myself, yourself and at least one other who we must decide on quickly. Our charitable purpose is for public benefit and community development and I have also prepared the detailed document for that. Again, your copy is in the file."

I gulped down the last mouthful of my drink, put down the cup and said, "Wow. You haven't wasted any time have you?"

He laughed and said, "Time's expensive. I'm keen to optimise those funds when we receive them. We need to put in place all necessary documentation to qualify for monetary relief."

"You mean, tax relief?" I asked.

"That and other considerations. It's all in your file."

I handed over the precious David Blakeney artwork for safekeeping. He placed the portfolio case in a strongbox container, closed the lid and put it in his personal safe. He drew our meeting to a close by informing us what amounts of money Eric had set aside for Mum and me. We weren't expecting that. We listened in absolute silence, unable to find any suitable words. In shock, we shook hands with Julian Hartley and, still dumbstruck, we made our way out. Mum and I left the Fairclough offices in a daze and stood on the street looking at one another.

"Did you understand all that stuff about setting up a charity?" Mum said eventually.

"Some of it. It's quite complicated, though isn't it? I'll need to study all that information. I'm sure Julian knows what he's doing but I need to know what I'm doing as well."

"Are you going back into work now, Rosie?"

"No," I said. "I've taken the day off. I thought we might be tied up much longer."

Still neither of us referred to our legacy. We walked along the High Street from the offices of Fairclough, Fairclough and Hartley and into a café. We didn't mention Eric's generous gift until we had more coffee and cake in front of us.

"I'm completely gobsmacked," Mum said.

"So am I. It's going to take a while to sink in."

We were both in a convoluted state of mind. A fierce mix of emotions made it hard to think straight. In spite of grieving the loss of our dear friend, we were elated by Julian's last piece of information. Until that moment I hadn't realised it's possible to feel sadness and joy at exactly the same time.

Chapter Thirty

It took a full six months to put together the Myrtle House charitable incorporated organisation by which time probate had gone through on Eric's will. His house on Emerald Street sold quickly and it gave me an uncomfortable feeling imagining other people living there. Somebody else would be in the kitchen where he used to give me those chocolate muffins. Some new person would clip the hedge at the front and hang out washing in the rear yard. I dreaded the thought that they would rip everything out and replace it. It was irrational of me but so much of my young life had been spent there it was difficult coming to terms with it. But Eric, bless him, had taken such good care of me and Mum in his will.

As well as bequeathing to his family, Eric had set aside generous amounts for us too. As executor, Julian Hartley had explained to us how it was all going to work. My mother decided she would use her legacy when it came through to pay off most of what remained of her mortgage. Keeping a smaller amount unpaid would avoid a large redemption fee. With the rest of the money she decided to buy a small second hand car. Paul offered to help her choose and go with her to view and test drive. It had been a long time since she'd driven. She admitted she felt nervous about it. It was great to see her making plans for the future. Paul and I decided to use ours to add to our savings and get out of our rental. We would put down a healthy deposit on one of the new builds on the rise overlooking the river.

An anonymous purchaser from New York bought the exclusive, previously unseen David Blakeney painting with its handwritten message from the artist himself. The event took place on an evening, ticket only sale organised by the auction house specialising in fine art. Apparently, the upcoming sale had set the art world on fire. The auction room was full. The door was locked against public entry. Champagne and canapés were served to the people present in their evening dress, seated on their gilded, red velvet chairs.

Early bids came from the floor, mostly from art dealers hoping to make a profit from selling on again afterwards. When the floor fell quiet, interested parties called in their bids on telephone lines from around the world. The eventual purchaser wished to remain unidentified and instructed that the winning bid also must remain undisclosed. People in the assembly room had heard the auctioneer call out the previous, earlier bids so had a good idea how vast a sum the anonymous bidder must have offered. Newspaper columnists could only guess at the final amount.

Now we knew we could go ahead with our plans for Myrtle House, but first we had to find a suitable plot.

After Eric died my mother didn't want to go back to working in the supermarket. She said she wanted to do something that had more meaning, more satisfaction. The supermarket where she worked before was offering her only short, part time shifts and, since she had no responsibilities at home other than herself, she felt there was much more she could do with her time. When Sylvia Midgeley retired and went to live nearer her daughter and grandchildren Mum took the job of warden at Myrtle Court. She was in her fifties then, still fit and active and, after her time with Eleanor and Eric, it was the ideal position for her. Accommodation came with the job, a bungalow like John's so she rented out the house on Emerald Street to a young couple just starting out. She told me she loved her new job and she'd never in her life felt so financially comfortable.

All the readers from the first group of Treasure Islanders have their own stories to tell. Andy Bishop's is one of my favourites. He told me how he first fell in love with one of the registered nurses he met while visiting John in hospital. She had a smile that made his stomach flip over, he said, a feeling he'd never experienced before. It was immediate. He watched her gentle, caring way of talking to John and explaining how they were helping him to get better, quelling his fears. She was so patient, an angel in a navy blue uniform. Andy was thoroughly smitten.

The trouble was, Alice was already engaged with the wedding only a few weeks away. Andy was heartbroken. He never forgot her. For years he kept his feelings about Alice to himself until one day he bumped into her in Morrisons supermarket. They went for a coffee and she told him how the marriage had lasted only fourteen months. Her husband had wanted to continue living a bachelor lifestyle, she said, and expected her to do everything at home as well as working full time at the hospital. Apparently, she eventually told her husband she had no intention of spending the rest of her life being his mother and that the marriage was over. She wanted a divorce. He wouldn't give his consent. He said he would argue against her interpretation of what constituted unreasonable behaviour. He told her that wives were supposed to do the housework and why should she be any different. According to him, every judge in the land would agree with him. She should think herself lucky he never laid a finger on her. He tried to convince her she had no grounds for divorce. So, she gathered up all her belongings, moved out of their home and rented a flat. He continued to refuse to give his consent. At the time, divorce regulations required a term of five years separation without the consent of the other if there were no other grounds. Alice was seeing out the five years separation rule and just getting on with her life which, according to what Andy told me, was happier without the lazy, entitled Mama's boy she didn't know her husband was until after she married him.

In nineteen eighty five Andy Bishop married his Alice Parsons. You can imagine how many times they had their legs pulled over that name change. Their wedding at the Parish Church in Kingsley was beautiful and joyful. I was twenty then, still at university but I came home for the wedding. A couple of years later I was godmother to their first child at the baptism in the same church.

W.P.C. Sarah Wilson went to Manchester on her promotion. P.C. Colin Radcliffe went to the West Midlands force. Jackie Nelson became section and then managing editor of the Kingsley News before she went to Yorkshire Television. I sometimes see her name on the credits after some big national story scoop.

Michael Drummond is in his eighties now and still taking photographs. There's a permanent exhibition of his work in the Myrtle Park museum. Yorkshire Television did a documentary about him and how his local wildlife pictures had gained popularity nation wide.

Recently redundant Stephen Whitlock, who hadn't read a book for years and brought his dog Yogi to the first Treasure Island readers' group meeting at the tuck shop in Myrtle Park, retrained to achieve his heavy goods vehicle driving licence. He landed a job with a multi-national long distance haulage company driving goods throughout Europe. He must have liked what he'd seen as we heard he bought a place in Spain and took his family to live there.

Molly Stott took over the Treasure Islanders' meetings on evenings when Mum couldn't do it. She was the biggest bookworm of all and always credited Eleanor Hewitt for igniting her passion for reading. She became a much admired, loving foster parent in Kingsley and helped many children and teenagers through difficult times in their lives.

Many more Kingsley people added their names to the Treasure Islanders group and all of them wrote their notes for the growing collection of reasons for taking the book to read. Mum kept them all, carefully stored in an arch lever file. I didn't meet most of these new group members while I was away at university but Paul and I joined in occasionally once we'd settled in the area.

The last year of the old millennium brought two surprises. Paul and I had given up hope of having a child of our own. We'd both had all the tests. There was no medical reason why it hadn't happened. I taught myself to stop thinking about it, stop longing for what might-have-beens. Then, I learned I was pregnant. At thirty five I also learned I was considered an elderly primigravida. Elderly at thirty five? I remember thinking that, surely, they could come up with a less insulting description of someone my age expecting her first baby. Naïvely perhaps, I wasn't aware of the risks. Mum was over the moon. She admitted she'd thought she was never going to have the fun of being a grandma. She was ready to shop for baby clothes already. She also expressed concern.

"I know you love your work, Rosie," she said, "but why don't you take a break now? What does Paul say?"

"Same as you, Mum."

"There you are then. We only want what's best for you."

"I know, Mum."

"Eric would have been so proud of you. Chief librarian. How fantastic is that? But if he was here now he'd say the same as me and Paul. You know he would."

"You got me," I said. "Psychological blackmail, mother. I can't argue with that."

She laughed and said, "I'm prepared to say and do whatever it takes, Rosie."

I handed in my notice. Our son, Josh was a new millennium baby, born in February two thousand. He grew up more interested in computers than books. Currently he's doing important research into the further use of artificial intelligence in medical sciences. The mind boggles just hearing him talk about the coming revolution in health care systems. Eleanor Hewitt would have loved to listen to what he knows.

During the same week as I learned I was pregnant with Josh, the old Kingsley further education college suddenly came up for sale. The college had been converted from an elegant Edwardian mansion in expansive gardens. Courses under the auspices of Bradford University were moved to different locations, either within the university campus itself or at Ilkley College fifteen miles away. The local council invited tenders. As one of the trustees of our newly formed charitable organisation I went along with the others for a viewing. We were seven in number: Julian Hartley who had with him our proposed project manager, the Kingsley mayor, the chair of our council, plus representatives from the charities Helpers and The Tomorrow Charity founded in Liverpool, and myself.

We met first at the offices of Fairclough solicitors where Julian had laid out preliminary architect's plans for the future Myrtle House. Although there might have to be adjustments made to the original design depending on the plot size and aspect, the plan nevertheless illustrated the scope of our intended facilities.

The old college was situated on the other side of the river from Myrtle Park in an elevated position facing southwest in grounds that rose from the river bank through a wooded area and up to terraced lawns surrounding the building. It was impressive. The access road approached from the rear of the mansion house and turned one way into a large car park and the other way around the side of the building and into the drive at the front. Someone mentioned walking, mobility scooter and wheelchair accessibility.

"It would be a simple matter to create a pathway through the trees to the river," the project manager said. "It isn't much more than a stream at that point. In fact, there used to be a ford there back in the old days. For horses and carts going to market, you understand. A small footbridge would lead straight into the lower field of the park. From there it's easy access to the centre of town."

Heads nodded. Faces lit up with smiles. Promises were made for support with our bid for the property. We left feeling confident.

The metropolitan district council preferred our plans from those of our main competitors, a development company wanting to use the plot to demolish the old mansion house and build modern, luxury apartments. They emphasised the fabulous views once most of the trees were removed. We put forward a strong case based on our benefactor's wishes to provide facilities for young adults with special needs so that they could live a more independent life, assisted by a small team of skilled supporters.

Our plan outlined keeping the original college building and creating new dwellings to provide living accommodation similar to the bungalows at Myrtle Court where each unit would have its own fully appointed kitchen. There'd be gardens and vegetable plots, seating and quiet areas, and a barbecue pit and outdoor dining facilities under an open sided barn- like structure. The main building would keep its exterior appearance but be almost gutted inside. The ground floor would house communal rooms for group activities, meetings and an exercise room with specialised equipment. Offices would be on the upper floor as well as extra bedrooms for temporary and respite guests. All spaces would be accessible to wheelchair users including a specially designed lift.

The proposed plan for twenty five permanent residents plus the respite facility was accepted. We held a ground- breaking ceremony in August. The work was completed in June 2001 and we appointed Andy Bishop as manager. The first residents moved in almost straight away including John who, having had a look around, thought it would be good for him to be with people nearer his own age. He was forty six then and still working a few hours daily in Myrtle Park with the new Chief. I didn't like to tell him he was growing nearer the age of some Myrtle Court residents than the young people at the House. I knew he was suspicious of change but agreed he would enjoy making new friends. He was concerned about all the elderly residents at Myrtle Court and how they'd manage their gardens without him.

"There's nothing to stop you going over there to do the gardens if you want to," I told him. "You don't have to stay at the House all the time."

He considered that for a moment with a frown on his face. Then he smiled and said, "I'll be spoiled for choice of places to go, won't I?"

"Yes, you will. Mum would still be happy to see you at Myrtle Court."

"I forgot about that," he said. "Mrs Linda likes me to pop in to see her on my way home. I could still help her with the Saturday morning shopping as well."

"And at the big House, Andy will be there every day during the week."

"Yes, he will. I like Andy. He's helped me a lot. We get on very well. What about all my things though? I have my special things. I can't leave them behind. And my house plants. How will I get them there?"

"I'll help you to pack up, John. Don't worry. We can take our time and do it all bit by bit."

"You have Josh to look after," he said.

"Can't he come and help as well? He loves putting things in boxes including himself."

John laughed and said, "Yes, we can give him his own box to sit in." He frowned again and added, "what do you think I should pack away first?"

John had just started having a few working memory problems. Mum mentioned there were times he seemed forgetful or he wouldn't be able to work out how to do things he'd done a thousand times before such as organising his gardening tasks and in what order to do them. Moving into Myrtle House would mean there'd be more people to keep an eye on him as his own needs increased.

Chapter Thirty One

It's been a glorious, high summer day in August, twenty five years since the groundbreaking ceremony for Myrtle House. Today we've celebrated the anniversary. We had a huge marquee in the gardens and put the barbecue to use. The seats in the open barn filled with residents, families and guests listening to live music. Andy Bishop is in his seventies and retired now from managing Myrtle House but he volunteered to help staff with the grilling. There was nothing over fanciful. All the residents had ticked their preferences on a list in the communal lounge so sausages, burgers and chicken drumsticks made up the menu for the day. Mum, now in her eighties stood beside Andy and fried onions for the hot dogs, till her legs ached and she had to sit down.

The gardens and surrounding grounds at Myrtle House looked amazing in the sun. We were able to spill out from the marquee onto the grass and into the shade of surrounding sycamore trees. I heard somebody say it's been almost like a royal garden party at Buckingham Palace. Everybody came in their Sunday best. Julian Hartley came with the mayor and her husband and she gave such a great speech commending the work we do here and how it all began.

I've taken a heap of photos to show to Jenny next time I visit her at Myrtle Court. If, and it's a big if, I can get a word in. She is truly amazing. Ninety eight years old and sharp as a tack. The only time she's quiet is when she's listening to news about John. She loves to hear how he's doing and often reminisces about her time running the old tuck shop in the park. John tells me when he goes to visit her she enjoys going over all the same subjects while he's eating the chocolate cake she makes for him.

Myrtle House is a special place. You could call it magical. That wouldn't be an exaggeration. It wouldn't exist if not for Jenny, Mum, John and me, but most of all Eric whose generous gift provided the funds in the first place. We all played our part in its creation.

Who can say where the magic really began? Was it when a little girl made friends with a lonely young man with a rare medical condition? Was it when an absentee father unknowingly made way for another man to become an honorary grandfather? Or was it when another single mother bought her son a book he couldn't read just because there was a character called Long John in it? Did it begin with a student artist leaving one of his college books on a train?

Inside Myrtle House, the manager's office where I work now has a star-shaped name plate on the door. 'Eric's Place' it says. Our residents always ask about him and I tell them his story. If you should ask any one of them for their address they wouldn't say Myrtle House. They'd tell you they live at Eric's place. It makes me happy to hear them say his name. After all, this is *his* place.

On the wall in the office is a printed copy of an exceptionally special painting of Myrtle House. The viewpoint is from above so you can see the path running down through the trees to the river and the footbridge into the bottom field in Myrtle Park. It was signed and donated by the artist David Blakeney. How he came to hear about us we can only guess. On our tenth anniversary he sent us a letter admiring the work we do here and letting us know how much he loved the way we came about the funding to begin this much needed facility. He donated the painting of Myrtle House some months later and said it was for 'if you ever need further finances'. I did wonder then whether he had been the unidentified purchaser of Eric's artwork. The original oil painting of Myrtle House is safely lodged elsewhere. It belongs to the charity.

As well as residents' families and representatives from the council we invited Molly Stott and current members of the Treasure Islanders. It isn't an incongruous mix. Eric was a founder member of the reading group after all. It's been a pleasure to re-connect with familiar people and share how we've all managed through the years after austerity, a global pandemic and yet more hardship.

Not all of us survived. We've lost Jill who brightened all our meetings with her nostalgic stories of when she was in the army and afterwards, how she became a martial arts instructor. Amanda's gone too. She'd always turn up to our monthly meetings with her latest batch of home made jams and pickles. Phil the joker is sadly missed. He filled every gap in awkward conversations with his comic tales. He lifted bad moods. You couldn't stay cross or angry with someone for long with Phil around. We all have bitter-sweet memories of those we've lost. We very nearly lost John too, all those years ago.

Now that the guests have all gone I'm happy to sit and put my feet up and relax. I've taken the armchair by the patio doors and I can see the House team clearing away.

"You like working here, don't you, Rosie?" John says. We're in his room with cups of tea and biscuits: chocolate, of course, and he's asked for the story of Rosie and John. He's taken his usual place on Eric's old sofa. That sofa is older than me. It took us a long time to persuade him to have it completely re-upholstered. He swears it's the only sofa that will ever be comfortable for him. We managed to win his approval by finding a William Morris style fabric almost identical to the original.

"I do like working here, John," I say.

"Better than when you worked in the library?"

"Oh, that's a tough question. You know how much I love books. I enjoyed my work then. Now I love my work in a different way."

"What way? How is it different?"

I knew John wouldn't be satisfied with a generalised comment.

"I enjoy working with people," I tell him.

"Is it because people are like books?"

"I'm not sure what you mean, John."

He grins and says, "Books have stories in them. People are like books because they have stories in them too."

"Oh, John. That's perfect," I tell him. "I couldn't think of a better way to describe it. Thank you. Yes, we all have our own stories to tell. Everybody here at Eric's place has a story worth the telling."

"Where was Josh today, Rosie? I didn't see him," John says.

"He's working in the Netherlands now, John," I tell him. "He couldn't get away today but he's coming for a visit at the weekend."

"I remember Josh when he was a little boy."

"You had some good times together, didn't you?"

"Yes. He liked my old comics. He's all grown up now. Do children always grow up so fast, Rosie?"

"I think they do."

"Yes," John says. "I remember you as a little girl too. You grew up fast. Did I grow up fast as well?"

He had his seventieth birthday last spring and it isn't easy finding the right words. He's the oldest resident at Myrtle House but still feels he isn't ready to go back to a bungalow at Myrtle Court now that Mum doesn't work there.

"You did, John. And as we grow older time seems to go by faster than ever." I say.

"Oh. I wondered if it might have been different for me. I've always known how it feels to be different."

"Yes, I know, John," I say. "Would you like to talk about that now or do you want me to carry on with the story?"

"Of course I want you to carry on. Go on. She was an only child comes next."

It isn't long before he interrupts again.

"We worked it all out together, though, didn't we?" he says as he reaches out for another chocolate biscuit.

"We did," I say. "I couldn't have done it without your help."

He nods, pleased with the memory and satisfied with his own part in it.

"Just a minute," he says. "In the parts of the story where it's about Eric or Jenny or somebody else, how do you know what they did or what they said? You weren't there with them."

"Ah, that's a really good question, John. They told me their side of the story so I had a good idea how to put it together. I had to use my imagination a bit. I've read a lot of books so I know how to do that."

"Hmm. You were always full of ideas. Go on," he says. "Rosie was a serious child is the next part."

And five minutes later, "I remember the old streets and the way Kingsley used to look," John says. "So many of those old buildings have gone now, haven't they?"

We slide out of John's favourite story and talk about Kingsley the way it used to be. We grieve for the things we miss and criticise town planning for the things we believe haven't improved and we wish they'd left alone.

We reminisce about John when he was a young man and Eric and Jenny when none of us had any idea that a ten year old girl who wanted to bring magic into other people's lives could actually make it happen.

And so, I'm ready to slip back into the narrative when John shrugs his shoulders and grins at me. He gets up from Eric's old sofa and picks up the now empty biscuit plate.

"Tea's gone cold," he says. "I'll make some more."

"I'll come with you."

We take our mugs into his kitchen and I run some washing up water at the sink while he reaches for fresh teabags.

"I was a funny youngster, wasn't I?" he says.

"So was I."

"But you helped me."

"So did you."

"There's another pack of chocolate biscuits up here," he says, stretching over me to get into the wall cupboard. "Give me a minute. You take the tea in and carry on with the story. More about Eric comes next."

I go back to the armchair and put the mugs on the table. I can hear him brushing biscuit crumbs into the waste bin, then the rustle of waxy paper as he opens a new pack. He comes back with a clean plate and four biscuits.

It still surprises me that John is never openly offended by talk of his condition yet he prefers to hear our story as if we were characters in a book. I used to think he was in some kind of denial, afraid of facing up

223

to the truth of his history, unable to come to terms with the facts of our lives. I know different now. I believe it's his choice to talk about it as if it was fiction. He knows that everything I tell him really happened but, for him, separating the truths of our past, real lives from our bodily selves in the here and now creates an element of mystery and, I suppose, re-creates the magic we hoped to make. He likes to hear about himself in the third person. John in the story can be a different John from the one who, years later, sits on his sofa slurping tea and eating chocolate biscuits. And it's okay. He knows the real truth. He's also aware that I know he knows it. As soon as he's settled again I carry on.

"What happened to those roller boots, Rosie? Have you still got them?"

"I grew out of them, John. My feet got too big. By the time my broken ankle mended and I was strong enough they didn't fit me any more. I think my mother took them back to the charity shop."

"The roller boot day was a special day," he says. "I remember everything about it."

"Oh, so do I. I remember the feeling of excitement I had when I saw my birthday present. I couldn't settle at school. All I could think about was learning how to roller skate. It was such a special gift. I thought my mother must have worked some special kind of magic of her own to be able to afford to buy them. I didn't find out until later that they'd come from the charity shop, but even if I had known then it wouldn't have mattered to me. I was absolutely fizzing with joy."

"You were very excited?"

"Yes, John. That day was a turning point in all our lives, wasn't it? Life changed for every single one of us but it was only the beginning. We didn't know where it would lead."

"We know now." he says. "We were the first people in the whole world to leave a book on a park bench, but nobody knows that, do they?"

"It doesn't matter, John," I say. "What matters most is we found a way to make new friends."

It also isn't important if we don't finish the story of Rosie and John today. He'll remind me where we left off the next time I see him. Anyway, the story isn't finished yet. We'll be friends for ever and who knows what might happen next. I look at my watch. There's another hour yet before Paul comes back to pick me up.

"What would have happened, Rosie, if I'd lost my book?" John says.

"We'd have used a different one."

"Ah, but then it wouldn't be the same people who wanted to read it."

He's right, of course. Treasure Island was the only book with the power to bring Eleanor Hewitt into our lives and into the story of Rosie and John, the Treasure Islanders and Myrtle House. The book we chose to use came about through luck rather than management. That is, unless the god of putting things right had something to do with it.

THE END

A message from the author-

I hope you've enjoyed the read as much as I enjoyed writing it. I'd be so pleased if you would spare a minute to write a review for Amazon and/or Goodreads to help me reach more readers. Just a couple of sentences is fine. Thank you.

Books by Celia Micklefield

<u>Novels</u>

Patterns of Our Lives
Set in Yorkshire and Norfolk from 1935 to 2009. A dual timeline historical saga. Audrey Freeman was a ten pound Pom. When she returns to England she discovers secrets from WW2 that she was never meant to know. (some sexually explicit scenes)

The Sandman and Mrs Carter
Set in Wiltshire. A psychological/medical mystery. Feeling neglected by her husband and missing her sons at university, Wendy Carter worries about her mother who is showing symptoms of dementia.

When her mother makes a miraculous recovery, changes in the Carter household become impossible to bear.

A Measured Man
Set in Norfolk. A not-so-romantic comedy. A bachelor in his fifties, Aubrey Tennant is still looking for his ideal woman. He relies on well-rehearsed phrases to attract ideal candidates. When he meets Lisa Miller he believes he's found The One. He doesn't know she's already buried two husbands.

Rosie, John and the God of Putting Things Right
Set in 1970s Kingsley, Yorkshire. A random act of kindness conjures magic. Friendship between a ten year old schoolgirl and a disabled young man overcomes negative attitudes and instigates changes that last a lifetime.

Serial

Trobairitz the Storyteller
Set in France. A dual narrative cross genre novel ideal for book clubs. At an overnight truck stop a contemporary trobairitz (female troubadour) begins the telling of a story about 'love that is beyond most human understanding'. Her themes, like those of the original medieval trobairitz, reflect issues

causing problems in her own life: tradition, culture, relationships and the role of women in society.

Trobairitz -her story continues
Book two in the series brings more conflict, scandal, a wedding and a funeral.

Short story collections

Arse(d) Ends
Stories inspired by words ending in the letters a.r.s.e. There aren't many in the English language. Themes include annoying habits, sexual harassment, dysfunctional relationships.

Queer as Folk
Stories about love, loss and life itself.

American Tan
More stories of life, loss, love and nostalgia

Nonfiction

People Who Hurt
Memoir.